other titles by james d. mccallister
available from Mind Harvest Press

King's Highway
Fellow Traveler
Let the Glory Pass Away
The Year They Canceled Christmas
Dogs of Parsons Hollow
Dixiana
Down in Dixiana
Dixiana Darling
Mansion of High Ghosts
Reconstruction of the Fables
Ironically Unreal Once Forever

The Night I Prayed to Elvis and Other Stories

James D. McCallister

Mind Harvest Press

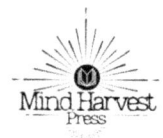

Copyright © 2024 by James D. McCallister

All rights reserved.

No part of this book may be reproduced in any form or by any electronic or mechanical means, including information storage and retrieval systems, without written permission from the author, except for the use of brief quotations in a book review.

This is a work of fiction. Names, characters, businesses, places, events and incidents are either the products of the author's imagination or used in a fictitious manner. Any resemblance to actual persons, living or dead, or actual events is purely coincidental.

ISBN: 978-1-946052-54-4 (Hardcover)

For more information:

Mind Harvest Press
PO Box 50552
Columbia SC 29250-0552
www.mindharvestpress.com
www.jamesdmccallister.com

contents

Author's Note	ix
Face at the Window	1
Armageddon Afternoon	18
Trailer Trash	44
The Night I Prayed to Elvis	59
Spin the Bubble	82
Heroes and Villains	94
Earworm	104
Eye of the Vandal	119
I Puked at Karoake	131
The Blogosphere Version	138
Release into Prayer	155
Trauma and Restoration	184
Button, Her Sister, Their Father, and Lucky Latham	204
The Fable of Samson & Trudy	208
Travis Latham, A General, and a Vietnamese Girl	219
Acknowledgments	234
About the Author	235

author's note

Nothing pleases a writer more than seeing his children finally grow up and get out of the basement. As with my prior story collection THE YEAR THEY CANCELED CHRISTMAS, I've lived with some of these pieces for quite a long time—most all were written in the years 2003-2009. Long enough to have given up hope that they would ever see publication. The rejections arrived swift and numerous on many of these stories.

I first teased the idea of a "Lucy and Timmy Latham" collection on my author website a full decade ago, during my high, fine season as an author on the verge of breaking out: a new book, my second, in print, an agent attempting to sell a third, plus interest from an academic press in yet another manuscript. I posted many paragraphs extolling the virtues of not only what I'd already produced, but all the volumes of material to come for any enterprising publisher willing to *take a chance* on this burgeoning, forty-ish late bloomer.

The best part? All the books supposedly to come were neither wishcasting nor an empty boast; by this point I had written a million words. More. I had stacks of pages in multiple drawers, so to speak.

During that championship season came a fine finish for a particular short story close to my heart, a finalist award from a once venerated American magazine who, in their words promoting the announcement of the winners, had published many of the great literary voices of our time. Now, I was to be one of them.

Unfortunately... those other wonderful developments earlier noted failed to come to full fruition. The agent failed to sell the book, after which she dropped me; the academic press waffled for over a year before bailing. But no one can take away my short story awards and finishes. Those moments of positive feedback gave me, and give every writer, the steam to keep on with what is, overall, a thankless and painful journey.

Nor could they prevent me from pressing on with my own publications, which has become the standard today for many talented and ambitious authors who may have played the publisher's row game and lost, or simply never bothered in the first place. In my case the birth of Mind Harvest Press, as well as the many digital tools available to any writer with a computer, made all dreams come true.

As such my imprint continues to offer an outlet for work brand new, such as my 2023 poetry collection IRONICALLY UNREAL ONCE FOREVER, or this, my second story collection, containing many pieces close to the heart, and on which I attempted to cut my storytelling teeth. Feels good to publish a book a year. But those days may soon come to a close, as the stash of material dwindles and I leave behind the long fiction project which consumed my heart, mind and soul for so many decades.

In learning to write evocative, character-driven fiction I did what the experts suggested: I wrote what I knew. Most of these stories are thus taken directly from personal experience;

and if it wasn't my experience then courtesy my generous wife, who lived on that bend in the road out in the countryside. (Or, where my own imagination and experience fell short, seedlings for stories taken from memories and tales confided in me by assorted friends and loved ones—we daren't call it thievery, now, shall we? Surely not.)

The voice in the story will be POV-close of either Lucy or Timmy; some of these are attempts to write in the voice of the child at that age, others are of the older self narrating back. In those days I wrote many stories in a variety of voices and genres, but the personal nature of most of this work required a particular approach which ought to be apparent from the introductory lines of 'Face at the Window.'

As for the bonus material from the DIXIANA series, it seemed apropos to include excerpts featuring Lucy and Timmy's dad Travis "Lucky" Latham, who we learn went to Vietnam with two other Edgewater County friends, one of whom failed to return. Also included is a second of several appearances in my Edgewater County series by the mythic, mighty figure 'Samson' who makes a memorable appearance here in one story.

Thanks to all who inspired this work, and to you who now read it on your visit to fabled and storied Edgewater County. If you're new 'around here,' not only are there plenty of other stories and novels set in this fictional county, these make for as good a place as any of the books to start. Enjoy your stay!

JAMES D. MCCALLISTER
WEST COLUMBIA, SC
FEBRUARY 20, 2024

"Cultivate the art of bestowing the devotion and love which we lavish on distant and unreachable beauty also to the beauty which is close and familiar."

Hermann Hesse

face at the window

THE NIGHT I SEEN THE AWFUL FACE AT THE WIN-DER happened right before I got in trouble at school over not knowing how to do my math right. I woke and seen it looking in at me—a monster.

I screamed and hollered. The round moon-face disappeared.

Daddy come running down the hall, asking what on earth was the matter.

I told him about the face outside, looking in at me. "I seen it *right there*."

Daddy ran to the front door and put on the porch light. I heard him stepping around, crunching in the oak and maple leaves he kept putting off raking into a big pile.

With the porch light on, I did not feel near as scared. I sneaked over to the win-der to peek outside.

Daddy stood in the front yard, looking out over the small rise toward the bend in the road we live on, the corner where the bus picks me up to go to first grade. He turned his flashlight this way and that.

He came back in. "Sissy, it couldn't've been nobody.

Them's sticky holly bushes under that window of your'n. Ain't no footprints in the clay, neither."

"But I seen someone." The words wouldn't hardly come out! "*A face at that win-der,*" I said all breath-y.

"Sugar, mercy. You just had a bad dream." His sleepy face turned cross. "And look here, I want you to quit saying 'win-der' like that. It makes you sound like a redneck from over in Red Mound."

I didn't understand. "Don't *you* call it a win-der too?"

"The word is *win-duh*. You seen a face outside your *win-duh*."

"But—I thought you said it was just a dream?"

He got mad. "Go on back to sleep. I mean it—I ain't asking. I got to be up for work in two durn hours, girl."

Daddy, he works early. Sometimes he's home by the time the bus drops us off from school, on most days anyways. Not all the time, though. He works overtime a good bit. Mama went back to work too, once I started school. We stay with Mee-maw at her house until Mama gets off at five and comes to get us. Daddy's home by then, but this way he don't have to mess with us without Mama at home.

He pulled my door shut. I could hear Mama's voice asking what on earth was going on. He mumbled something I couldn't understand.

Peeking out from under my soft blanket, I tried not to look out the window. Daddy had left the porch light on at least, which helped. But I couldn't go back to sleep, not with the thought that a face might appear at the win-*duh*. I kept hearing sounds like footsteps, then I realized it wasn't nothing but my own heart beating inside my ears.

Finally, gray light started coming up and I heard Daddy's noisy work belt, the one with the metal buckle like he wore when he was in the army, back before I was born. It jingle-jangles when he puts it on. If you's awake in our house when he gets dressed, you hear the belt. And then the clink of the coffee cup, his spoon stirring in the cream. A little while later, his truck engine rumbles and durn near vibrates the whole house. And he's gone.

Daddy never does eat him a good breakfast before he goes, even if Mama has made biscuits—he always waits and gets him a stale day-old donut or bear claw from the store, which for him is free. He says it's one of the best reasons he likes to work at the IGA: he can get breakfast for nothing, long as it's day-old and headed for the big brown trash bins behind the store.

I wonder if his free breakfast is like when we went into that gas station on the way down to Myrtle Beach last summer? And how, while Daddy was paying the old man for our gas, I watched Timmy take himself gum and a candy bar and put them into his pocket? Since I figured it was okay, I went and took myself a roll of Sweet Tarts. I reckoned the candy was free for us kids, like Daddy's breakfasts are for him. Timmy's my big brother. He's smarter than me, about two-numbers and all sorts of stuff. I do what he does. Most of the time.

TIMMY HAS HIMSELF A MEAN STREAK, though. Lying in the bed worrying about the face at the win-duh, I remembered him and his werewolf mask. Back when I wasn't but three, Mama bought Timmy the mask from the Woolworth's in downtown Tillman Falls, right before Halloween that year. That's when I was a pixie with wings like Tinkerbell. But not a fairy, a pixie, which I kept having to explain to the folks handing out candy.

For a solid week before trick or treat time, Timmy ran around wearing that mask. Halloween way out here in the country don't amount to much—Mee-Maw's house and my aunt Minny and the Pirkles down the road. That's about it. So I reckon he was trying to make the most of it.

Thing was, I knew the werewolf head was only a rubber mask? But it still scared the mud out of me? Timmy would take it off and shake it in my face. The mask, with long hair and a red tongue lolling out over its bloody rubber fangs, gave me goose-implies—the bad kind, on the back of my neck.

"I think this creature's gonna come and look *right into* your bedroom window tonight," he told me on Thursday before Halloween. "*That's vat I think,*" trying to sound like the man on TV who hosts *Thriller* on Sunday afternoons, the old monster movies from back when everything was black and white.

I went and cried to Mama. She hollered at him to quit telling stories, and not only that but to come take out the trash for Mama, "like a big boy, now."

That night I couldn't sleep for minute, not knowing that a monster with red or maybe yellow glowing eyes, and hot breath fogging the window, and a bloody horrible tongue hanging out, was peeping in at me.

I kept calling for Mama. She had her hair in curlers and said for me to quit with this mess and to go to sleep. I told her I had a tummy ache. I even let her give me that nasty pink Pepmo Bimsall twice—twice!—just so she would come back in one more time.

I peered out from under my quilt a couple of times. I didn't see nothing at my window. Not that time.

THE NEXT AFTERNOON we was sitting on the back porch while Mee-maw and Mama shelled peas, and Mama was talking to her? Like I wasn't there? Mama don't know that sometimes? When I'm in the floor playing and humming to myself, I'm actually listening? I just didn't usually understand much of what they said. Grownup stuff, usually about some mess Uncle Junior had gotten mixed up in.

Mama said, "Sissy had me up and down all night. I swear she did not sleep a blessed wink."

"What was wrong, angel?" Mee-maw asked.

"A woolly-booger was gonna come and get me." Just saying it made my stomach drop and feel all dizzy in my head.

"Well, darling. There ain't no woolly-boogers. You been watching too much of that durn television."

Timmy, who had been sitting on the steps having himself a cold root beer, busted out laughing until the drink gushed out from his nose. And he kept on laughing, too, until I was so mad I ran over and threw my dolly at the back of his head. Hard as I could. It's fine. She's plastic.

He cried that it hurt. Boo-hoo. He made such a fuss Mee-maw ended up taking a switch and popping us *both* on our bare legs. She told us that if we did not settle down, she might have herself a thrombosis. I did not know what that word meant.

ONCE MAMA GOT us up I tried to get out of school, saying I was sick.

She didn't believe me. "You're just tired from them bad dreams of your'n."

I went to school. When I saw it was the substitute teacher,

I started to shake all along my insides—her face looked like the one at the win-*duh*.

Miss Sweinsteiger—a name so weird and clumsy I could not even say it proper—looked like a cross bulldog, fat and hateful, and with a mustache on her lip. She seemed younger than Mrs. Stewart, who was old like my Me-Maw. Miss Sweinsteiger seemed too young to have got so mean already.

"We're doing math today." The substitute, her ugly face looking all swole up with fat, pointed at the chalkboard. "Look up yonder at them equations. Write them down and fill in the answers."

I giggled at chubby Roy Earl Pettus, who lives in the house down near the pecan orchard on River Ridge Road, up past Mr. Glasscock's farm with its rows of cotton. Roy Earl does not have parents, only grandparents, which I still cannot figure out! We're friends from the bus ride, but not like boyfriend-girlfriend.

"Hey, Lucy." Roy Earl's face turns pink as my pillowcase at home. "I'll help you if you need it."

"Thank you, that's sweet," I said, and he turned pinker.

But Mrs. Sweinsteiger hollered at me to hush up and face forward, so I did.

I wished I hadn't—when I looked up at the board, I knew what she had wrote went way over my head.

She looked right at me, too.

Like she had planned it this way.

Like she had it in for me.

Like she was a monster.

With my hand shaking I wrote down the numbers and tried to add them, but like before, this was harder than what I could understand from when Mrs. Stewart had taught us. This was two-numbers, and I can't do two-numbers yet. Just can't feature them.

But I ain't no dummy, so I set to trying again. I scrunched up my mouth and tried, but I could not figure out how to add up or subtract the stacks of two-numbers. I don't do good with math no way—I much prefer learning to read, which is more like fun time, like when Daddy reads Little Golden books to me and Timmy, or used to. Timmy's too old for that now.

"I can't do it," I said when the teacher came to check on me.

"You keep trying, Lucy."

"But I don't know how to do two-numbers yet."

Her fat face turned red. Compared to our regular teacher, she was acting like the devil. Her breath stunk like rotten onions. *"You'll sit there until you quit pretending you don't know how to add up them numbers."*

I cried and cried, but I could not add them together right. One-numbers, now, those I could add. But not two-numbers like eleven, which I wanted to say as 'eleben.' Dang if that ain't not-right either.

My tears started dripping onto the paper and smeared the two-numbers, making them even harder to understand. Some of the boys snickered and laughed. I kept trying and trying, but I couldn't think straight no more. The harder I tried, the less I understood.

Even some of the girls laughed, but not Darlynn, who's my friend since forever. We ride the bus together every day. She looked mad, sticking her tongue out at the substitute when she waddled by the line of students to open the classroom door and let them go out to play and have fun at recess.

While I was left sitting there. Crying.

"You ain't going outside with the rest of the class till you add up them numbers." She leaned down, whispering. I half expected the wicked substitute to have on the striped socks like the wicked witch under Dorothy's house.

I could not help myself—tears kept bubbling over like grits cooking on a too-hot stove. It was like I had got stuck while everyone else had moved on. I was trapped there at that table along with them cursed two-numbers.

Next thing I knew the class all lined up, putting on their jackets and hats to go outside and play. Fall was here. It always made me sad when the weather cooled off, mainly because fall meant school again.

They stood snickering and whispering and pointing. I did not look at them, rather, I could see out of the corners of my eyes. I sat still, like a stone. My insides were shaking, and tears kept sneaking out, but I sure did not want them to see that I was a big baby.

The class went outside. I was left there alone.

Worst of all, I needed to pee.

You can guess what happened from there. That teacher left me sitting there all through the next period, crying and sniffling and staring at the two-numbers and starting to hurt down yonder, until I cried and begged to please go to the bathroom. And she relented, bark-bark-barking at me like an ugly bulldog.

But when I got up, I didn't even make it out the door before I started peeing on myself.

Everybody started hollering and pointing at the floor. I cried again, hiding my face.

I SAT in the nurse's office on a chair that seemed harder than normal, waiting for Mee-maw to pick me up since Mama and Daddy was both at work. I had passed by the janitor, who looked glum as he pushed his mop bucket along back toward Mrs. Stewart's classroom, where if she had been there, none of this mess would have happened.

The nurse came in, a big black woman with a mole hanging off her neck named Miss McCaskill. She had given me a little boy's shorts, way too big. They had pockets, though, which I liked. I kept my hands in the pockets the whole time I waited in the nurse's station. I played with lint until it made two little balls that I pushed down into the deep corners of the pockets. I wondered what little boy had lost his shorts, and what had been in his pockets, and then I worried that these had been peed in by a little boy, and my stomach started feeling sick.

Mee-maw arrived, walking down the hall toward me, the sunlight from outside behind her. Her arms were outstretched to me. I started crying again. I ran over to her.

"Well, darling. What's wrong?" She asked if I was sick.

"No, ma'am." Shamed, I told her in bare whispers what had happened, how I had had to sit by myself for a long time working on them two-numbers.

"What on earth do they have you wearing?" She grabbed at the shorts, mumbling and cussing like she does when she's cross. Her hands, especially her nails, were dirty—she must've been in her garden when the nurse called. No wonder she was mad.

Mee-maw looked me all up and down. "Wait—*Mrs. Stewart made you sit there till you pee-peed in your drawers?*"

"No—it was Miss Sweinsteiger."

"*Who?*"

"She's our substitute teacher today."

Mee-maw said a bad word under her breath. "Sissy," which is what the family calls me half the time, "you sit back down on that bench and don't move, not till I get back. You hear me?"

I told her I did.

My grandmama went stomping into the office where the principal sat. Words was flung around I did not understand. Nothing unusual there. Mee-maw's voice had gone all high and screechy—it sounded like it did whenever Uncle Junior pulled some of his shenanigans.

You don't mess with Mee-maw, not once she's mad. One time? She cussed my uncle bloody, after I went out back to where his trailer sits and found him with a girl.

They were in the bed. The both of them didn't have on no pajamas. When I come in they had been laughing and rolling around under the sheets with both their feet sticking out—dirty feet. Junior didn't never clean up that trailer of his.

I hollered for them to *Quit wrestling*. This startled them both like I was a ghost, or had on Timmy's werewolf mask.

"Sissy, get back out yonder," Junior said from under the sheet. "Go on, now,"

"That better not be *your* little girl," I heard the naked woman say. She sounded snotty and mean, like her poo-poo didn't stink.

"Shit, no—it's my sister's." To me he said, "Go on now, sweetheart, before I pop you. You knock before you come in somewhere."

"I did. Y'all just didn't hear me, wrestling like you was."

"Hush your mouth. You did not knock," the woman said.

I stuck out my tongue. Her boobie, all big and flabby, peeked out at me from above Uncle Junior's yellow sheets. "Get on, now," my uncle said again.

I told Mee-maw. Once I did, she had rushed out there stomping her feet in quick little steps like she done going into the principal's office, outside of which I waited, listening to the hot words flying.

When she came back out, Mr. Quattlebaum, the assistant principal, stood beside her and smiled all toothy at me. He asked me to explain exactly what had happened. His bowtie, jug ears and jiggling loose neck made him look like a dressed-up frog.

Same as to Mee-maw, I said how Miss Sweinsteiger done me the way she done.

"I see. And when you told her you had to—" His face turned red as Roy Earl's. "Go to the bathroom?"

"Yes, sir?"

"She didn't let you?"

No, I heard myself say. I cried again, ashamed and hot all over. "Not until I did the two-numbers, but I kept telling her I didn't understand. And then I couldn't hold it no more..."

"Don't move a muscle," he finally said. "We'll be right back."

Now both went stomping down the hallway together.

AFTER A WHILE, Mee-maw returned alone. Now she was sashaying instead of her cross little fast footsteps. "Let's scoot on back to the house, Lucy. And get you into your own clothes."

In Grandddaddy's big blue Cadillac Riviera, I asked what happened.

Mee-maw lit up one of her cigarettes and frowned real hard, like she had a bad headache. "I got that durn little so-and-so fired on the spot, Sissy. For doing that to you. Like she ain't got no damn sense."

The closer we got to home, the more Mee-maw started coughing and holding her head.

"You all right, Mee-maw?"

"I think I got so hot and bothered I give myself heatstroke."

"Even though it's chilly outside?"

She turned on the air. "I'm hot all over," she said. The vents blew back my stringy hair.

AT HOME we went up onto the porch and into the house. She was fussing about wanting to get "a durn stranger's" clothes off me, she said, while still coughing and holding her back like it was hurting. Mee-maw told me to go get a dress and shorty-shorts for myself out of the room where we kept things for me and Timmy. We stayed there after school and in the summer.

"Go and wash yourself in the bathroom, too." It was like she didn't have no breath, like when I felt ashamed trying to explain what had happened to make me pee in my drawers. "I got to go lay down. Put a cold cloth on my head."

She belched, big and long. It sounded like when Daddy drinks him a beer on Saturdays while him and Junior mess with one or the other's dumb old car, or the Ford pickup Granddaddy keeps in the back yard for taking trash to the dump. "Oh, that's better. A little."

I done as she asked. While I did not see her with a cool cloth on her head, she did go and lay herself out along the couch, face down, coughing and going *oh-oh-oh* under her breath. I just figured she was tired.

Face at the Window

AFTER I CHANGED into a little pink dress and a light blue sweater, because it was chilly in the house, which is old, so much older than ours, I heard Mee-maw call for me to come back into the living room. She had rolled over and lay on her back, her arms crossed over her chest.

"Go out back and see if your Uncle Junior's home from work yet." She squeezed her eyes shut and belched again. "Go on, now."

I went to go get him.

"Wait—run in there and get me the big turkey pan. It's under the stove in that big old drawer."

I ran and yanked on the greasy handle. The heavy drawer full of her biggest pans and broilers scraped out onto the kitchen floor. I got what I thought was the turkey pan and ran back in.

"Put it on the coffee table." Mee-maw sucked in her breath real sharp. "Now run and get Junior," but I couldn't hardly hear her—she started throwing up.

Right into the pan.

In the living room!

I got scared.

Right as I busted out the back door, I heard Mee-maw moaning again.

A voice kept yelling in my head:

You peeing in your pants made Mee-maw sick. You two-number dummy!

Mercy, but I was glad when I got outside and seen Junior pulling up. Before he could halfway get out of his hard-top GTO, I hollered at him:

"*Mee-maw's laying on the couch and throwing up all over.*"

"Do what, now?"

He cussed and said he'd come inside in a minute, after he had a shower—he was all covered in grease from where he worked on cars up at the body shop.

I started bawling. I begged him to come right now. Mee-maw hadn't ever been sick in front of me. Don't nobody want to listen to no little girl, I reckon, but he done as I asked and followed me inside.

After Junior came into the house and seen her on the couch, he turned white as Mee-maw looked. With his long skinny arms and legs going every which way, he run and snatched that phone up so fast it was like in a cartoon.

Mee-maw had quit coughing and belching. She had gone all still and quiet, taking a nap. It made me glad to see she had settled down. I felt relieved.

About fifteen minutes went by till the ambulance got there. Uncle Junior made me sit out on the porch. He wouldn't let me go back inside, not even after Daddy arrived. He kept telling me, "Mee-maw's sleeping. Mee-maw's sleeping."

It didn't sound true, somehow. I felt strange inside. Cold and empty and sad.

About the time the ambulance men got there, I heard my Daddy start boo-hooing inside the house. Well, dang. This had turned into the strangest day there ever was.

AFTER A LONG TIME of worrying myself to death over Mama all evening, who kept on crying the way Mee-maw had been coughing and belching, they made me go to bed. The house had been full of people for hours.

Daddy came into my room, his eyes all red and shiny.

Face at the Window 15

"You understand how Mee-maw's done gone away from us. Don't you?"

I told him I reckoned I did. That earlier today, she had seemed so very asleep.

"The sleep of heaven. She's up there right now, trying out her wings."

I said I thought that sounded good. "When's she coming back?"

The way he looked at me, he didn't have to say it. But he did. "She ain't, honey."

A hard and hurtful knot welled up inside. I couldn't catch my breath. Daddy held me tight. He kissed me on the head and hummed till I got back my wind.

"You want me to leave the light on?"

Big girls didn't keep the lights on. That's what he told me a hundred times. I thought about the face at the window. But kept it to myself. "No."

"Okay. Sleep tight—you're Daddy's earth angel, you know."

I told him I did know and that I was glad.

I ROLLED AROUND. I kept feeling as though I had drifted off, but my dreams were so busy! All night long Uncle Junior kept running in the room, and Mee-maw was belching, and it was like the TV from in yonder was at the end of my bed with heads and mouths going jibber-jabber. Voices. My Mee-maw's white face.

I woke up crying. I looked at the window.

Suddenly President Nixon looked inside at me, talking with his big old cheeks and jowls and sweaty upper lip like he had been on the TV earlier tonight. And the President Nixon face started talking right at me, but it was all scary like a Frankenstein's monster, going MM-MM-MM HUH-HUH-HUH, and I looked again but now it was her—Mee-maw—instead of the President. No, really—my Mee-maw's face, all white and big and looking inside at me.

This ain't no real thing; this is a dream, and please to the good Lord that I may wake up now.

I screamed. Good and loud.

Daddy come a running and flipped on the light, saying he knew this was bound to happen.

"I seen a face at my window again."

"Not again, sugar."

"Uh-huh. This time it was President Nixon."

He stood looking at me all blank. He laughed. And kept laughing. He leaned against the door frame, wiping his eyes. "Well I done been all the way to the State Fair and halfway around the world in the service, but I can tell you ain't no President Nixon out there."

"Oh, but Daddy... *I seen it.*" I decided to tell the truth. "And then it turned into Mee-maw." I cried.

He hugged me, crying too. "Go back to sleep, honey. Wa'n't nothing but a dream... today was an awful dream."

In the dark I tried not to think about Mee-maw, and with my eyes shut good and tight I drifted back off.

THE NEXT MORNING, I tried to think through what all had happened. I kept trying to understand how it was Mee-maw would not wake up, and never would again.

I sat eating biscuits and honey, listening to Mama and them talk about Mee-maw's funeral. Half the words I couldn't understand, especially when Daddy got out his adding machine, called the funeral home, and started messing with two-numbers.

Mama kept on sniffling, but not crying as hard. Not as much.

Not quite.

I peeked over Daddy's shoulder while he added the numbers, squinting at the tape coming from the adding machine. Boy howdy—what he was figuring on? It wasn't only two-numbers, but also three- and four-numbers. I was glad he had that adding machine, because if you asked me to add them up? I couldn't've done it to save my durn life.

Now, numbers? Them is something worth being scared over. Not some face at the win-*duh*. Especially if ain't really there. Not if it was my Mee-maw's face, which I would never see again, because they didn't let me see her in her casket that weekend. They said I was too little for all that.

Mama quit work after all that funeral mess and dealing with the house, mainly because we didn't have no one to keep us after school no more.

I kept crying over Mee-maw for a long time after, especially on Fridays, which was when we would go over and have her special fried chicken. Somehow I knew I never would taste chicken that good again, not even after I learned one day how to make it myself.

For a time I would look at the old photo album with Mee-maw's pictures and wish she could come back. One day, I didn't seem to cry no more. I had got used to her being gone, I reckon. I worried that I was wicked for not feeling sad like I did, but I never said nothing to anyone about it. All I could do was hope this was a normal way to feel.

armageddon afternoon

On the second day of Easter week, you wouldn't have found anybody more happy than me to have a break from riding the school bus all the way into town. Worst part of third grade. Out in the country where we live, it sometimes takes an hour to get home in the afternoon. I can't wait for summer.

But Tuesdays, whatever the season, seem boring any way you cut it. You know we'll eat hamburger steak with fried onions and gravy for dinner, and Mama and Daddy will watch *Hawaii Five-O*. Come to think of it, most of the days of the week are predictable like that. Mondays are *Gunsmoke* and pork chops, with Mama getting her ironing done. Only thing different lately is that we don't go to Mee-maw's on Friday for her chicken anymore—Mama fries it here, and Papaw comes over to eat with us now that he's alone.

This Tuesday turns out different, though. Boy, does it ever.

Out of the blue, our Uncle Junior—a hellion, in my mama's words—comes by, a surprise, to take us riding in his GTO. As he goes sliding onto our dirt driveway off the main road his loud muffler sounds to me like it's broken, but he swears it's supposed to be that noisy. Don't make good sense. Today that muffler plumb-near rattles my teeth, one of which is already loose, the last of my baby ones. I don't feel any more grown up, though, especially since everyone still treats me like a baby. "Little one," my mama calls me. I'm ready to be big, so I can have the grownup glass of sweet tea instead of the small ones they give me.

Uncle Junior—his real name's Gareth, but nobody calls him that—didn't have much else to do these days but ride around. Right after the first of the year, he got laid off from his job at the body shop.

Cars cars cars. That's all he talks about and messes with. Says he's gonna start his own car shop one day, with three big mechanic's bays and "the whole shebang," as he puts it. His fingernails are always dirty with grease, and he loves to cut the fool. That's Uncle Junior.

Mama and Daddy talk about how he needs to get him a new job before long, before he starts getting into real trouble. What kind of trouble I do not know, other than having no money from not working, which far as I'm concerned sounds like trouble enough, at least to an eight year-old girl from out in the sticks of Edgewater County. It's all anybody talks about —money, money, money, and how to get some. That part of being grownup doesn't sound too fun.

Around the time Uncle Junior gets out of his GTO, the tornado siren over near Red Mound also starts going off —*whirr whirr whirr*, way off in the distance. Them fellas down at the firehouse test it out all the time to make sure it works; it's like the noise that comes on in the middle of a TV show sometimes, or in a song on the radio, making an irritating high pitched sound and a man's voice saying "*This is a only a test of the Emergency Broadcasting System.*" After a while nobody paid no more attention to them announcements, because the time for needing them never seems to come. At least not to me, anyway.

Daddy says they also test the siren so often because we got the Sugeree River Station, the nuclear plant—Daddy says it 'nu-que-lar' but my teacher Mrs. Simon claims that ain't right—which might blow up one day, or some other awful thing. Only last year, men in yellow DOT trucks had come through on our road and put up signs that read EMERGENCY EVACUATION ROUTE. The sign at the end of our road reminds me of the one on the side of the high school gym. There, it's on a fading yellow square of tin from the 1950s, ages ago, and which reads FALLOUT SHELTER.

Uncle Junior came running onto the porch. He didn't look like he had either one of his oars in the river—his eyes were all bugged out, sweating. He looked downright scared. That ain't no kind of expression I ever seen on my uncle's face before.

"Y'all hear that siren?"

"Yes sir, Uncle Junior. Clear as day."

"Well, we got to go," he said, breathing all hard. "It's the end times that's done come. *Lord have mercy on our souls, children.*"

I thought he was gonna bust out laughing, but he didn't. Fact is, he fell down on one knee and bowed his head like we was in church. "Lord deliver us," he whispered.

Goose pimples all over my arms. I feel scared.

Junior, skinny as a scarecrow and with a big old head of frizzy coarse hair sticking out from under his hat, has fuzzy sideburns and a thick mustache that droops down the sides of

Armageddon Afternoon   21

his mouth. He likes going around with girls—one time when I was real little, I went out to his trailer behind Mee-maw's house and seen him play-fighting under the covers with a woman named Angie. They had wrestled so hard their clothes had come off!

Timmy, eleven and still with his babyfat, puts down the funny book he's been reading and sounds all smart-alecky. "That ain't the siren for no end times coming. I wish you'd quit telling stories," something we'd heard my Mama say a hundred times about our uncle.

Junior springs up like a pogo stick, brushing the yard-dirt off the knees of his greasy jeans, which stayed dirty from working on cars so much, like his fingernails. "I ain't kidding, boy. Now y'all get in the dad-gum car... *while we still got time.*"

We all stand there.

"Now!" Junior hollers, making us jump.

Okay. He ain't never raised his voice to me before, except maybe when I caught him wrestling with that girl and he shooed me out. Now I know my uncle's serious.

But I'm not sure what to do—Mama's gone down the hill to the Pirkles to get some fresh eggs from their chickens. They had a deal going: Mrs. Pirkle swaps eggs for our squash and tomatoes, which will come in later in the season, over in the sun-facing side yard where mama grows her vegetables.

Mama! The thought of leaving her behind is worse than whatever Junior thinks is happening. "*We got to wait for Mama*," I yell loud as can be heard.

"It's too late for her," shaking his head and tsk-tsking, taking his hat off. "I'm sorry, little angel."

Timmy's face goes as pale as one of Mama's white sheets hanging damp on the clothesline. "Do *what*, Uncle Junior?"

"Oh—what I *mean* is, I seen your Daddy down the hill,

told him what was going on, and he done went and got her. We going to meet them right now, over at the church. And you know who else we gonna meet, don't you?"

Timmy and I stand frozen, our mouths hanging open. "Jesus? My voice has gone little.

"The battle of Armageddon is being waged overseas even as we speak. The Lord is nigh, children. He's a-coming back. And then we're leaving this world," sweeping his hand all around at the woods and the road and the steep hill where the branch runs and I like to go and sit by myself sometimes just to think, "to be taken home to the Promised Land."

We let this news sink in.

"What about our *stuff*?" Timmy's eyes bugged out now like Junior's. "I ain't gonna leave all my toys."

Junior started to grin, which seemed strange if the world was ending. But then, they do tell you in church how it's going to be right nice once the Lord comes back and carries His flock on up to Heaven with Him.

"Where we're going, nobody ain't gonna need no footballs or comic books or TV sets, not ever again," my uncle explained. "Not once we're driving on the streets of gold."

"Driving? You mean you get to take your car?"

"Don't you know how Heaven works, son?" He shook his head. "There'll be a golden eight-cylinder Dodge Challenger, with leather bucket seats and a tape player and modified with nitrous-oxide injection, warmed up and waiting for us."

Far as I knew Junior hadn't set foot in church before or since Mee-maw died. Not that I've ever seen.

The siren in the distance went off, finally.

"Oh, dear Lord." Junior, bowing his head. "Would that thy grace preserve and keep us safe from the demons lurking out yonder." He spat over into Mama's flower bed. "Now come on, young'uns."

I started crying. Timmy looked both scared and mad at the same time, somehow. His face had gone from white to red. "What about *buh-buh*-Buster?" Buster's our hound dog. We keep him tied up out back. When Timmy's voice broke I knew he was fixing to cry, too. "We can't go without Buster."

"Well-sir: I reckon you better go rustle him up."

Quick as can be, Timmy's running back around the house, but Buster's already way ahead of him, pink tongue flapping and smiling that doggie smile he gets whenever we let him off the chain to run around or go riding in Daddy's truck, which we do every other Saturday when he's off from the IGA. On them mornings Daddy likes to run us over to the new Hardee's by the interstate junction to go through the pull-up window. He gets us all steak biscuits, even Buster, who don't normally eat nothing but kibble, so to him chomping down on one of them greasy biscuits must seem like the downright bee's knees.

At the GTO, which is orange on its body with one of them hard black vinyl tops, Junior made us wait until he could take a big yellow beach towel and spread it out on the backseat for Buster to sit on. I didn't know why. If we wasn't going to need none of our things up in Heaven—or wherever we was going—Junior sure shouldn't worry about his car seats staying clean.

Did we get to keep the things we loved up in Heaven?

The things we carried in our hearts?

Golden versions?

"Sissy," which is what they all call me instead of my given name, Lucy, "you sit up front with me."

Uncle Junior cranked the car; the muffler seemed louder than ever. He took off his Redtails ball cap and shook out his frizzy hair. His eyes darted all around. "I'd be fibbing to y'all if I didn't admit how I'm about scared enough to mess my drawers. Yes, I am. But, look here—we got to go. We got to try. Lord help us."

Timmy busted out crying. I joined him.

"*Boo hoo hoo*," my uncle said, wiping his eyes. "It'll be okay, y'all. Praise Jesus."

On a dime, though, he quits crying and fires up a cigarette and throws that car into gear. We peel out of the yard, kicking up gravel and pebbles and probably a bunch of Timmy's marbles, too, from where he plays in the dirt. My uncle floors that gas pedal and goes tearing around the bend toward the highway, fat black tires squealing and dust going everywhere, a huge cloud like in a war movie when a bomb goes off. It ain't rained worth a durn toot this spring so far. Mama says she's gonna run the well dry with all the watering she has to do.

I lay against the car door, still heaving and crying. Buster, panting and sticking his head out the window like dogs always do, seems so happy. Timmy's leaning his face down into Buster's dirty brown fur. I think my brother's crying again.

Junior finally says to me, real quiet, reaching across and locking the door. "It's gonna be all right. Jesus will protect us."

That makes me feel better. "I sure hope so."

"Ain't no need for hoping," he says, winking, "when you got faith."

WE DROVE hard on the back roads of Lynch's Crossroads and halfway to Red Mound, or so it seemed. Houses and trees and all the pretty azaleas blooming zoomed along besides us. Mama had been excited because a Grandaddy Graybeard in the back yard had flowered so pretty, she said, despite the dry weather.

The sun's out.

Birds, singing.

There ain't no more sirens.

Or other folks zipping around in a panic about the end times being upon us all.

That's when I start to think Junior might be cutting the fool with us like he always does.

I thought to myself: if Jesus *was* going to be coming back today, I reckoned the sky ought to be all purple, or on fire, or some such calamitous development. Everybody I seen, though, standing in their yards watering flowers or riding in other cars, didn't look like they was readying for the Rapture. Nope. They're going about their business like on any ordinary Tuesday here in Edgewater County.

We come to a stop sign. A fat old lady in a flower-print housedress, standing on lumpy feet on the front porch of a tin-roof house set back from the road, smoked while eyeballing us in the street. She holds a greenish-black hosepipe wrapped around her arm like a snake, spraying out into the yellow dry grass of her yard.

A Big Idea to test the truth of Junior's story: "Maybe we ought to see what the *radio* says about Armageddon."

"*Hmm.*" Junior, pulling at his mustache and pitching his cigarette butt out the window, nods at me. "Maybe we ought to."

Turning on the radio, he punches through the buttons. All the stations run music and commercials like normal. After stopping on WABA, he lets 'Palisades Park' by Freddie Cannon play and even turns it up.

Uncle Junior, drumming his fingers on the steering wheel

in time to the music, shrugs at us. "I reckon they don't want to scare no one just yet."

"I reckon not," I said.

"You're full of bullcrap!" Timmy, slapping at the vinyl seat, has turned red. "You ain't got good sense, Uncle Junior."

"You might not be the first to tell me that, son," bugging out his eyes. "Maybe I ain't got good sense. But what I do have, my children, is faith in the Lord above to keep me and mine safe from evil."

With a solemn air in the car like at church on Sunday, he peels away from the stop sign as the spring air, so sweet and warm, blows all our hair.

My uncle bumped his hand against the wrapped leather of his steering wheel and sang along until 'Palisades Park' ended. A commercial comes on for Mr. Vincent's Ace Hardware. They're having a spring sale on garden tools, it sounds like. Buster sticks his snout back into the car long enough to sneeze and blow dog snot everywhere.

Junior, scratching his chin, seems faraway. "Maybe that's how Heaven's gonna be..."

"Like how?"

My uncle downshifts onto a road I don't recognize. "Like Palisades Park."

I don't know what Palisades Park is like and say so; Junior explains it's a place like the Pavilion in Myrtle Beach, one of my favorite stops at the beach.

I slide over on the seat and cup my hands around Uncle Junior's ear so Timmy can't hear. "We ain't really going to meet Jesus—*are we*." I'm not asking. I already know.

Junior crinkles his eyes real sweet. "Why, sure we are, Sissy." He whispers, "Maybe not today, though."

Being in on his joke feels good. Grownup, like.

He revs the engine and works his gearshift, a black eight-ball like on a pool table. "Y'all wanna go a hundred? Might never get another chance."

His feet pump the pedals and we go faster. The car vibrates with power, makes me feel good and safe. The muffler sounds even more like he should get it fixed. The faster we go, the more Buster looks like the happiest dog the Lord's ever seen fit to make.

The old country road, which didn't have a house but every now and then, started curving. I stick my hand out the window. "This'd be a good way to catch a frog," I yell, saying what comes to mind whether it makes any sense or not.

"Yeah, Sissy. It sure would, sugar."

"I wish y'all would both just shut up," Timmy calls over the wind. I stick out my pink tongue at my brother, who ain't being nothing but a big old baby. He's mad. He's not in on the joke like little Sissy.

WE POP BACK out onto the highway not far from the crossroads where there's more houses. Junior rolls up his window and fishes a fresh cigarette out of a pack of Lucky Strikes from his shirt pocket, a denim shirt washed so many times now it's starting to look white. The pack is all wrinkled, looking like he's only got another one or two smokes left. Junior's always smoking, but Daddy only does once in a while.

My uncle tucks the cigarette in the corner of his mouth. "Y'all remember me telling you about Samson?"

Leaning forward, Timmy looked curious. "What about Samson?"

"Reckon we might ought to run up and see him. One more time," Junior said, snorting and pressing his lips together like he was trying to keep from busting out laughing, "before this end-times mess gets going good."

My brother sucked his teeth. "I don't think there really is a Samson."

"Okay, then," Junior said with a wicked look in his eye. "We better go and find out."

Samson, real or not, is supposedly this big biker who lives way up the ridge almost to Parson's Hollow, back in the woods not far from what everybody called Mr. Rembert's land, where all summer long on Saturday nights they put on dogfights and cockfights, which I hear that people come from all over to see and make bets on. Samson's part of the motorcycle club in Edgewater County called the Pagan Knights, and in earlier times Junior had a chopper and used to ride with them, until one night when Junior wrecked his motorcycle. After that he didn't want to ride no more. He had hurt his leg bad, and still limped.

Junior had told us that Samson was called thus because of being big and strong, and how people would come from all over and pay money to see him perform incredible feats—busting concrete blocks with just his fist, lifting enormous weights like an engine block over his head, even drinking battery acid. Junior said he'd heard how Samson once worked at a carnival sideshow like they got at the State Fair; they called him the Strongest Redneck in the World. Every October when we go to Columbia to see the Fair, the freak shows scare me—I walk right on by them things. I don't want to see no snake woman or glass eater or poor little cow with two heads.

Mercy. He was more than human, this Samson. A monster.

Right then I didn't think I wanted to go see Samson, the idea of which made me feel scared for the first time since

Junior come sliding into the yard and hollering about the end of the world.

"We ain't got time to see Samson, not with *you know* going on."

"But Sissy, who better to see before we see Jesus... than Samson?"

I didn't think Samson had much to do with Jesus, not based on what I had learned in vacation bible school last year, nor that I'd ever heard the pastor say anything like that.

Timmy yelled out. "I want to go back home." Buster woofed like he wanted to go home too, but on the other hand kept his head out the window sniffing at the wind like it was the best time in the world, so I doubt that's what he meant.

"Hurts to say so, but ain't no home to go *back* to. Except in the sky with Jesus."

"*Bullcrud*." Timmy's voice cracked like he was still scared.

"Son, you look-a-here." Junior, gearing down and rolling up to the next four-way stop sign, this one at the intersection where you turn to go to either Parson's Hollow or into downtown Tillman Falls, said, "Samson ain't gonna cotton to no little crybabies."

At this point it occurs to me that, since Junior's funning us about Jesus coming back—and I was pretty durn sure and all—what Mama will think when she gets back from the Pirkles to find us gone? She's liable to worry herself to death about us as it stood, especially me. She still won't let me go off by myself at the Belk's or in the grocery store.

And so, what's she gonna think about us being up the ridge at Samson's?

"I don't want to go there neither—I'm scared."

"P'shaw. Samson ain't nothing but a big-old teddy bear. Y'all can go play around his pond with Buster while I talk business with him. And maybe if y'all are respectful and brave, he'll show us how strong he is."

To get to Samson's, we have to ride through what I call the green tunnel, a real straight road with tall trees on both sides, the highway which goes beside the ridge that runs down one side of Edgewater County all the way to the Sugeree River.

Junior turns onto a dirt road going up the ridge and cuts over to a flat part. We pass by trailers and old shacks. Little barefoot black children and skinny dogs run around in dusty yards full of weeds and old cars.

We get to Samson's driveway and drive a ways back into the woods till we arrive at this old farm house, one that looks like it might fall over in a stiff wind. Cars, trucks, an old school bus, and motorcycles tore all to pieces sit everywhere, in the yard and the weeds and the woods.

Pulling around we see a garage building separate from the house made out of concrete blocks, with three bays. The biggest, broadest back I'd ever seen stands stooped over and messing around under the hood of a Camaro, the engine hanging on a big chain from a rig next to the car. An old barn over to the side seems worse than the house. A couple of barn cats lay in the sun licking themselves. I know Samson can hear us, but he don't turn around and stand up until after Junior parks and cuts off his engine.

Two bulldogs come running over toward us, growling. Buster starts barking and dancing around in the back seat, his paws scratching my brother's bare legs. Timmy cries out, "Ow, quit it, Buster—you're about to tear me to pieces."

"Y'all stay here." Uncle Junior, hopping out, does a funny little high-stepping march over to the big biker.

Samson claps his hands and cusses, but in a friendly way. After he hollers at them, the bulldogs go trotting back around to the side of the shed. I think Samson must stand a whole foot taller than Uncle Junior. Thick, kinky red hair is pulled back with a faded green bandana, with a red beard and mustache and nose-hairs sticking out to match; his jeans and his shirt, all covered in black grease, holds back the biggest, hardest looking stomach I think I ever did see.

Samson peers over at us in the car. "Dang, Junior—you brung young'uns all up in here? Who's them kids?"

"Them ain't nothing but my little niece and nephew. And Buster. I thought they could mess around down at the pond while we you-know."

Samson, glancing back at his dangling Camaro engine, grunts and spits into the dirt. "All right, I reckon. Lemme tie them dogs up first. If I don't, they might kill that one of your'n."

Buster sits panting and looking around. I figure it's good that dogs can't understand people-talk.

After Samson squared his bulldogs away in a pen we got out of the car, finally. All of us, especially Buster, have been getting mighty warm sitting in the sun.

Samson points over at his catfish pond way back behind the garage. "Y'all be careful back yonder. There's poison oak, and I seen a water moccasin earlier this morning big enough to swallow that old hound dog whole."

My stomach leaps up into my throat. "*You seen a snake?*"

"Aw, don't you worry, little sweetie," big ugly mean Samson says, not sounding all that mean. "You just stay your cute self on that path and away from the edge of the pond."

"Come on, Sissy." My brother goes on ahead, his head

and shoulders held up high. "Buster and me ain't going to let no snake get you."

"We'll be right along," Uncle Junior calls after us.

"I got puppies right now underneath the house, and it's time to teach them to swim," Samson hollers. "Y'all want to help me do that?"

"Yeah, I reckon," Timmy says, with Buster trotting on ahead of him. "That sounds cool."

THE POND IS STILL and quiet and beautiful. Dragonflies and other bugs go buzzing every which way right over the top of the water, sparkling with sunlight. In the pond float lilies and it's got green stuff over part of it. It's so peaceful back in here.

Samson has himself a good fishing spot all cleared, with a couple of lawn chairs and a dirty white cooler and a little plastic table with a big ashtray full of butts. Here the water is clear. You can see right down to the red clay bottom.

Timmy peeks into the empty cooler. "Shoot."

"What is it?"

"I just knew they'd be a mess of cold beer."

I put little fists on my hips and try to sound like Mama. "And what, pray tell, would you do with a cold beer?"

"I'd drink it. Like a man would."

Lord. What a load of manure. "You sure was crying like a big baby earlier. Not a man."

Timmy poked out his lips. "You know Jesus ain't coming back today."

"He might."

"Junior's just cutting the fool."

"He might *not* be."

Timmy petted Buster on the head. "Yeah, sure. Uncle Junior ain't never told a fib in this life."

After a while we hear voices: Uncle Junior and Samson are coming down the path. Samson's carrying a big cardboard box. A different brown dog with titties hanging down trots behind them. She's a mutt, one of those dogs who look like its legs ought to be longer than they are.

Junior's smoking again, but now it's a little wrinkly cigarette. Him and Samson hand it back and forth, which seems odd because I ain't never seen anybody sharing one like that. I reckon Junior didn't want to give Samson the last one out of the pack. Or something?

Buster runs over and barks, but the mother dog don't seem worried about him the way the bulldogs were. They sniff noses and butts. Buster snorts and kicks up dirt with his hind feet before running back over to us.

Junior sucks the smoke, which smells like lavender soap instead of tobacco, into his lungs and holds it there. "Goddog, beau," he says while trying to keep holding his breath, "that's the real deal."

Timmy speaks up. "What's that y'all smoking?"

Junior's eyes get real big. "Ain't nothing but rabbit tobacco."

"Do *what*?"

"Look here, boy," Samson says, "that's just my home-rolled smoke. It's cheaper than store-bought cigarettes. That's why it smells different. But forget all that mess."

He pulls the cardboard box open to reveal five brown puppies! They start jumping up, all squirming and falling all over each other. The mama dog sticks her snout inside the box like she's checking on them, and they all started jumping up to her.

"It's time these mongrels learnt to swim." Samson takes

the box over into the weeds where Buster stands sniffing. "Y'all each pick one of them up and come over here—there ain't no snakes this time of day."

Timmy and I both pick up a puppy, which makes the mama dog run back and forth yipping at us, her big teats flopping and swaying. Samson grabs himself another of the puppies.

Junior, his arms folded, stands watching us. His eyes have gone all squinty and red like he's fixing to boo-hoo. He keeps looking around behind him. "Feel like somebody's watching us."

"Watch me instead." Samson gently tosses his puppy, the little brown fuzzy ears flopping, through the air and into the water with a splash.

"*No,*" I scream—Samson wants to kill the puppies!

"It's okay, sweetheart," the big monster man says. "Look here, now—"

Sure enough, the puppy comes bobbing to the surface. His little dog legs work hard until he figures out how to swim. He makes his way out of the water onto the bank, shaking his fur and bouncing back toward his mama like a little brown wet turd with legs and ears.

"*He started to swim,*" Timmy says, excited.

"He sure did. Now y'all try it."

Timmy went and pitched his puppy way too hard, end over end. The little dog goes in snout first, and doesn't come back up right away. But when he does, he seems to swim even better than the first, all the way up onto the bank like he did it every day.

Still—I don't want to throw mind. I already love my puppy so much my heart hurts. I thought about calling him Brownie or maybe Pee-pot, considering the little yellow spot I just found on the front of my dress.

Pee=pot licks my face and my ear, tickling me. "I ain't throwing mine," I declare. "*Nuh-uh.*"

"Well, give him to me, then." Timmy grabs at Pee-pot. I hold on while my brother twists and pulls. The puppy yelps, loud and scared.

"Boy," Samson says, sounding stern like Daddy. "Let loose her dog."

"I want to throw it!"

"*Son*, you better mind me," Samson says in a voice made hoarse by all that rabbit tobacco. "Them ain't your dogs to mess with no way."

Timmy, whose eyes have gone big, lets Pee-pot go. I cuddle the puppy while the mama dog hops up to retrieve her baby from my arms.

Junior, mad as a snake at Timmy, goes to take another puppy out of the box, this one mostly black but with brown legs and paws. He tosses the little dog easy, much more so than Timmy. It goes in and pops right back up so fast it's like a cartoon. That's the dog who seems to like swimming best. He goes round in a circle with his little nose stuck up before paddling onto the shore, where he prances and shakes off water all around his mama's stubby mutt legs.

Timmy throws another one, this time more gentle like Uncle Junior and Samson , and that little dog also swims without any trouble.

"You sure you don't want your'n to learn to swim, little sister?" Samson smiles through brown teeth that need a good brushing. But he ain't no mean giant—he seems real nice, in fact.

I shake my head. "Mr. Samson?"

"What, sugar?"

"Can I keep him? *Please*? Buster is Timmy's dog, and I don't got one."

Samson looks to Uncle Junior. "Your uncle's got to decide that."

My uncle shrugs. "Don't make no difference to me."

All happy and excited and sure the adults are going to let me get my way, I do a little dance. "So I can have him?"

"Angel," Samson says. "He's all yours. He might be a she, though. We ought to look."

For some reason I figured they's all boy puppies, which once I thought about it, wouldn't make sense. You had to have boys and girls in a litter, or so I figured.

Samson holds him or her up and squints between the grunting puppy's wiggling, brown legs. "This here's a girl, all right."

"Yay!"

"I want one *too*," Timmy says in his jealous voice, like on Christmas morning when he starts messing with my toys as though his ain't good enough.

"You already got *Buster*," I tell him, kind of snarling like I'm a dog too.

"That's right." Junior's tongue makes a crackling sound when he talks. "I'm about thirsty enough to drank that whole blamed pond," he says to Samson. "Whatcha got cold?"

"C'mon, y'all—let's get us some drinks back up at the house." He puts the other puppies back in and picks up the box.

The whole house smells like their funny cigarette from before. In the kitchen Samson goes over real quick and puts what looks like an upside-down Frisbee full of little sticks into a cabinet.

We drink Pepsi while the men have PBR tallboys, talking about stuff I don't understand and people I don't know. Junior has to keep catching himself—he keeps starting to use cusswords.

My puppy sits on my lap until she falls asleep, her little brown ribs going up and down.

Samson finishes his beer faster than anyone I ever seen drink anything. He's big, I reckon, and can hold more than a normal person. He belches like he has a foghorn in his throat.

Junior finally says, "Mercy me, but I reckon we best head on down the road."

Samson looks right at me. "Y'all have fun today?"

"Yes sir."

"Yeah, I reckon." Timmy, still pouting about not getting his own puppy. "Better than Jesus coming back."

Samson shoots a look a Junior like *do-what?* Junior shrugs his skinny shoulders. "That boy's cutting the fool. Ain't you, Tim?"

Timmy frown at his uncle. Shrugs his own freckled shoulders.

Right then, Buster barks from outside. I bet he's saying 'I'm your dog, Timmy! Be true to me!' And maybe he did say that, in his own way. Ain't no way to know, is there?

IN THE CLUTTERED yard full of junk cars and car parts, Samson and my uncle shake hands, after which Junior puts another one of them rabbit tobacco cigarettes down into his shirt pocket.

"Mr. Samson?"

"What, Sissy?"

"Will you please show us how strong you are?"

Junior grins. "I told them that you're legendary, beau."

"Famous all over town? Might be all too true." Samson grunts, almost seems embarrassed. "You kids look here—if it was me, I wouldn't trust half of what this trash-talker tells you, and the other half I'd just ignore."

But Samson picks me up like I don't weigh no more than a bunch of kindling sticks. Like I don't weigh nothing.

"Hand me your puppy," Junior says.

Samson holds me up in front of him. "You ready?"

Somehow I know what he's going to do, which nobody's done since I was way little. "I reckon so."

Samson takes and spins me up in the air, higher than I've ever gone in my life, me twisting and turning like one of them Soviet Russian gymnasts on the Olympics. The trees and the sky and the clouds all go round in a blur. I spin, squealing and laughing, before coming back down into his arms, where he rocks me like a baby.

"That strong enough?"

"*Do it again.*"

And he does, twice more, until he says his arms is getting tired. "I ain't young as used to be, little Lucy Latham. And you're heavier than you look."

Giggling and dizzy, I almost lose my balance. When I can stand up straight again, Junior hands me back my puppy. "Let's run ourselves on home, children."

As we head out of his yard, Samson stands waving. He gives me a big wink. The mama dog and her puppies are at his feet, panting and playing.

"So," Timmy says in his smart-alecky voice, "we going to see Jesus *now*, Uncle Junior?"

"Y'all know I was just messing around."

"I told you," Timmy says. "Told you told you told you so."

"Y'all want to go fast again?"

"Yeah," my brother says. "Faster."

"Tell you what—put on them seatbelts, you hear?"

Seatbelt? "We ain't got one back here."

"It's stuck down in the seat. And—y'all hang onto them dogs."

Once we had finally messed with the seatbelts enough to get them fixed across our laps, we clutched Buster and Pee-pot close as Junior revved his engine and pealed out onto the highway. Almost to the long straightaway.

There ain't no cars coming either way.

He speeds up.

His muffler sounds louder than ever.

We come up to a fork. Junior cut the wheel. We jerked onto the dirt road, one running along Mr. Rembert's land.

Without warning my uncle yanked the emergency break and the GTO spun around twice, the world blurring and dust and dirt going everywhere. He let off the brake and jammed his gears and pumped the clutch and cut the wheel back in the opposite direction, and the next thing you know we're going straight again, real fast, kicking up a huge cloud.

"Whoa!" Timmy shouted, scared but excited.

Next thing, right as we were coming up on a curve, Junior slowed down some, but not much. "What y'all think about that? That was like one of them movie stunts—"

But he stops talking—the car's started sliding! The sand on the road here is loose and thick, where it washes down from up the hill.

Uncle Junior, downshifting, cussing up a storm, spins the steering wheel in the direction we're sliding. The GTO comes to rest sideways in the middle of the road.

None of us say anything at first. "Dang," Timmy finally says. "Let's do it again."

But before Junior can say anything our dust cloud catches up to us, like a sandstorm blowing in from the Sahara desert. "Crank up them windows," he hollers, but it's too late. Everything in the car, including us and the dogs, is now covered in powdery dirt.

We cough most of the way home.

"My sister's gonna be mad about how dirty y'all done got."

"Mama's gonna be mad no matter what," I tell him. "We been gone two whole hours."

"Shoot, Sissy—you're right." At that he punches the gas again, kicking up new dust and speeding us homeward.

Right before we get to our turnoff, we hear a *whoop-whoop* from behind us. A Sheriff's car has his blue and red lights going round.

We're in trouble! My stomach drops into my feet.

"Here we go," Junior says, cramming a stick of Big Red into his mouth and chewing to beat the band. "Y'all keep your mouths shut."

Dang if it ain't Sheriff Truluck himself walking up to the driver's side. The Sheriff's nowhere near as huge as Samson, but he has a gut and a mean face. "Boy, what is wrong with you? Step out of the vehicle."

"Sorry if I was speeding. I'm just hurrying my little niece and nephew home from getting a new puppy, Sheriff."

"Get out before I yank you out." He says it all real quiet. "You understand me?"

Junior climbs out. "Sheriff Truluck, now I know for a fact I wasn't going but five miles over. I even got them kids belted in snug and tight."

"That ain't why I'm pulling you over. Do you realize we got every deputy in this county out looking for them young'uns?"

"Oh, hell, y'all," I hear Junior say. "I just took them out riding."

"Why y'all covered in dirt?"

Junior told him the story of the slide, making it sound like it was a real accident, no fault of his own. "We was lucky to come out of the slide and get the car stopped, sir."

"So you're saying you been out *joyriding* with two little children?"

"It wasn't no joyriding—I wouldn't do that. I love them like they's my own."

"Son: you been drinking today?"

"No, sir."

"Anything else?"

"No, sir."

I suck in my breath. I can see the side of Junior's face kinda quivering. I know somehow that my Uncle's going to jail, and maybe us along with him.

Uncle Junior takes his hat off like he's showing respect. The puppy and Buster both are whining and restless.

"All right," Sheriff Truluck says. "Get back in and I'll follow you on up to the house."

Junior, pale and sweaty as we go down our road, drives real careful and slow and uses his signal, even when turning onto our property—he sure as heck didn't slide this time. As we got out Sheriff Truluck pulls in behind and switches off his bubblegum machine, as I've heard Junior call the blue lights.

Once she sees us Mama comes busting out of the screen door, hollering our names. Not a minute later, it's my Daddy's turn to come sliding into the yard in his truck like Junior done earlier.

Everybody converges in the yard at the same time. Buster runs straight back to his back yard without no one having to tell him. He goes right over to his water pan and starts pawing at it because it's empty. Timmy runs to fill it up.

Mama's face, red and splotchy, her eyes puffy, leans into my uncle. "Junior, have you lost your ever-loving *mind*?" Daddy offers a few exotic cusswords, some of which I don't quite catch.

Mama, finally collecting herself, turns her gaze on me and Pee-pot. "Oh, my lord—and where on earth did this puppy come from?"

I don't know how to answer. I hold Pee-pot close to me and lie. "I love her, Mama. We found her all by herself by the side of the river road. Please let me keep her."

"And you're both as dirty as Pigpen. You young'uns get in the house and start a bath running."

As we got in heated words are exchanged among the Sheriff and Mama and Daddy and my uncle—harsh tones, more cussing, with Junior sounding small and sorry. The Sheriff gets in his car, backs out and leaves.

Mama comes inside to help us get washed up. Daddy and Junior stay outside, where I hear more yelling.

"Uncle Junior didn't mean nothing by taking us riding."

"Timmy, you go in there and wash up first."

"Yes, ma'am."

"Give me that little angel," Mama says to me.

It hits me: "That's what I want to name her—*Angel*."

Mama puts my puppy down and holds me close. "I thought the bogeyman had come and took you away."

"It wasn't no one but Uncle Junior."

We both hear Junior's muffler start going *blop-blop-blop,* and then he's tearing out of the yard for the second time today, and without even telling us goodbye.

Uncle Junior doesn't come around much in the next few weeks, not even to cook out on Sundays. In fact, we don't see him again until the Fourth of July, when everyone, cousins and all, comes here to grill hot dogs and hamburgers and set off firecrackers. Nobody says nothing about the Armageddon Afternoon. Daddy and Uncle Junior get along fine, both drinking a cold beer while they poke at the sizzling meat on the grill.

Other than our dog Angel, who's getting big, it's like nothing happened. If the end times were coming for real anytime soon, life sure didn't feel like it. Not here in the summer after third grade, not while hearing 'Palisades Park' in my uncle's muscle car, with the wind on my face, a puppy in my lap, and my big brother Timmy by my side.

trailer trash

NOTHING SAID SUMMER LIKE THE END OF SCHOOL, and after 7th grade, no one was more ready than yours truly to be free of Ridgeland Middle, which prepared pimply, freckle-faced doofuses like me for James F. Byrnes High. At the beginning of the term I'd gotten into the only fight I'd ever had, which isn't worth recounting because it was only big dumb Andy Dworkin, a brute who picked fights with everyone, and by semester's end my heart had been broken by a would-be girlfriend, Shelby Fordham, so it'd been a season of conflict and disappointment. Far as I was concerned, the school year could take a flying leap.

In an annual tradition, that first week of June my grandfather took me down to the barber shop for us to get ourselves a trim, which we'd done each of the last two summers since he'd retired from the highway department. My folks both worked—daddy was produce manager at the Piggly Wiggly, and mama had gone back to work as a seamstress supervisor on the line at the hosiery mill; both of them were bossy bosses who acted that way at home, too—so in the summers I spent a fair amount of time with my grandparents.

For now. Soon, they'd have to start letting me stay alone after school, and all summer long.

Wouldn't they?

At Halsey's barber shop, I would see a different grandfather than the one I knew and loved. Here, Grandy—the other men called him Garland, his actual name—came off more relaxed and gregarious than around his adult children and their various rug-rats and yard apes, my cousins from one county over who'd visit on Sundays for cookouts and yard games and filial fellowship. Around the family, Grandy's was a taciturn and humorless presence, a private, tightlipped man inscrutably circumspect about making small talk. He seemed happiest sitting off by himself on the back porch, smoking and watching the sunset, alone but for the dogs. No one in the family appeared unduly concerned by the way he'd jump up from the supper or picnic table while still chewing his last bite of food, like he couldn't wait to get on with his business—or else get away from us all. Grandy. "He's just set in his ways," my grandmother would say in his defense.

One Sunday I asked Uncle Junior why Grandy kept to himself. He explained that Grandy'd suffered deprivations and horrors in the big war in which he'd fought—the world war they'd put on thirty-odd years before, one that men like Grandy and his barber shop brethren had all, seemingly, gone off together to fight. That, all these years later, he still suffered nightmares from what he'd experienced.

"Don't ask him to talk about it, though," my uncle cautioned. Uncle Junior was a joker, but about this he seemed deadly serious. "From what he told me, Grandy's seen things no decent person should ever see."

Not the best way to put off a kid whose imagination raced at the thought of a greater world outside Edgewater County, a boy whose curiosity simmered inside like a gas burner on low flame.

So, against his advice, I broke down and tried. When I went to cajole Grandy into talking about the war, though, he became angry, madder than I'd ever seen him. He cursed and told me to look it up in my school books. After that disturbing incident—Grandy was usually sweet and kind, never a cross word to me otherwise—I left the war alone.

IN THE BARBER SHOP, amidst cigarette smoke and newspapers and coffee and the smell of the blue antiseptic liquid in which the combs sat sterilizing, I flipped through a racing magazine and laughed at ribald jokes I didn't fully understand, including ones told by my own grandfather, using language I knew would never pass muster under my churchgoing Grandmama's roof.

Mr. Halsey had finished up with Grandy, who'd gone first in the chair. "Come on, punkin," he said, climbing down and shaking the barber's hand. "Get on over here and let's watch you get them ears lowered."

How he embarrassed me by using such a precious, babyish nickname. But even my given name—Timmy—sounded like that of a little kid, too. That's what being almost-thirteen's like, especially at Mr. Halsey's. There, I found myself surrounded not by other kids but old men who wore Vitalis in their hair, who still dressed and looked and acted as though it were 1958 instead of 1978. Who'd gone overseas, and killed Germans and Japanese. Meanwhile, at Halsey's Barber & Shave, I wasn't anything but a 'punkin,' one who still had his baby fat.

The sound of soft syrupy steel guitars came from the old

radio sitting on a shelf over the sink. WABA sounded the hour, and then the CBS Radio Network newsman came on, reporting what President Carter had said about the Soviet Union and the SALT talks. The old men ceased joking and began yakking about grownup matters. They cursed the ruthless, communist Russians and said things like *Lord have mercy, I hope one of these days we don't end up sending boys over yonder.*

"Ain't gonna be the Russians," Rabbit Pettus said, sucking his teeth. "No sir. This time it's gonna be us and the Jews against the Arabs and Persians, in the desert, and that's going to be the big war to end all wars. Read your Bible, fellas. It's all in there."

"P'shaw," Grandy said, "I'll be a monkey's uncle if you even remember the last time you got near the good book." This started off a fresh round of semi-heated discussion about war-making and world politics that I didn't so much not understand as not give a durn toot about—I was almost-thirteen. There'd be time enough for all that later.

Mr. Halsey pulled the cape around my neck, snapping it tight. He spun the chair so that I faced the large mirror. In its reflection I saw a panel of sage and wizened judges, the peanut gallery composed of my Grandy and his buddies all sitting with their legs crossed and heavy leather shoes on their big feet. Behind them, through the plate glass window looking onto the town green, were their cars all lined up: Grandy's brand new Riviera had been freshly washed, and with its slanted trunk appeared as a polished, angular royal blue shark of an automobile.

The barber contemplated my nubby noggin. "What say we give this young'un a buzz cut, like Sgt. Carter on *Gomer Pyle*?"

"No way, José," I said, which cracked him up. All my

friends had shaggy hair, shaggy as they—we—could get away with, and even sideburns for those of us whose whiskers were starting to fill in. "Like last time—just above my ears, please."

"Gonna be a hot one this year, son," Grandy advised, belching into a handkerchief he'd produced out of a pocket of his trousers. "I'd cut it short."

"High and tight sounds right to me," Rabbit said to a general murmuring of assent.

"*No*," I pleaded, embarrassed anew by my own outburst.

"All right, all right," Mr. Halsey said, patting me on the shoulder. "Don't let no one else decide what your hair ought'n to look like. Within reason, of course," he added.

The news ended and the next country song started up. The barber hummed to himself and began hacking at my undeniably unruly brown mop, which hadn't been cut since before Easter. Snip snip snip, auburn ringlets tumbling down to the black and white checkerboard floor; the toes of my Keds, worn and stained amber by the red clay of the riverbank where we'd gone fishing yesterday, peeked out from beneath the cape.

I thought about Shelby, who'd said she would meet me at the Spring Dance as my date, but then showed up holding hands with Cecil Waugh, of all people, a dumb football player chubbier than I was. My heart hurt, but it could have been worse—she might have shown up with Cecil's twin brother Harlem, the lesser of the pair in both looks and smarts. Despite the betrayal, I couldn't stop thinking about her.

"You know, what a boy like this needs," my barber said, pausing to take a thoughtful, deep drag from the cigarette he kept clamped in a wrinkled corner of his mouth, squinting down through the drifting smoke as he cut heads, "is somebody to put him to work for the summer. Good, honest work."

Rabbit—a giant of a man who owned The Dixiana, a restaurant and honkytonk across the green—agreed in his gravelly Carolina brogue. "Good honest work puts meat on a boy's bones. Character in the gut."

Burnham Sykes, who I thought of as the scariest, sourest man in Edgewater County, rattled his newspaper and sucked snot back into his sinuses. As he spoke, a loose turkey-neck jiggled under his chin. It made him look like a nasty freckled catfish somebody'd drug up out of the river. "What in the *hell* would you know about honest work, Pettus?"

"Kiss my behind," Rabbit said. I'd heard this kind of banter before, could almost recite it. They were best friends, Burnham and Rabbit.

"Burnie," my Grandy said, smacking Sykes on the leg with a rolled up *Field & Stream*, "I'm betting a man like you's got all manner of work for a young buck like this."

Sykes cut his eyes at me over the *Edgewater Advocate* he'd been perusing. He spoke in an aristocratic, low-country cadence which flowed lazily like a river, one untroubled by the passage of time it took for its statements to come to full articulation. "Matter of fact... I reckon I might would. Certainly. Work suitable for an industrious and healthy boy like Timmy... good, hard, manual labor... that is what's being suggested, here. Is it not?"

Everyone but me agreed that such endeavor was precisely what they had in mind. Nevin Pirkle Sr., blind and lame, rapped his cane against the tile floor. Everyone quieted. He intoned, "A wiser man than me once said, 'Work will make you free.'"

Murmuring and head-nodding. "If you say so, old fart," Mr. Halsey mumbled where only I could hear him.

Sounded like horse hockey to me, as Col. Potter on *M*A*S*H* would have put it. Only many years later would I discover the actual source of old man Pirkle's purported wisdom: an inscription that greeted doomed detainees upon their arrival at the iron gates leading into Auschwitz.

"I thought 'Manuel Labor' was the Mexican ambassador," Grandy quipped to general amusement. "But, no fooling—what you got for this little man to work on?"

I felt terrified, but also knew that having a job meant money—and if I had to work for Burnham Sykes, I intended to get paid. Money I could use to take a second stab at Shelby, ask her on a real date. The PG-rated *Saturday Night Fever*, an edited version re-released so that the pubescent Shelbys of the world didn't have to sneak in to watch John Travolta dance, was playing that week at the Palmetto, the marquee of which I could see sitting catty-corner across the town green from the barber shop. "How much you gonna give me?"

He put down his paper, smacked his fish-lips and smiled crookedly like a villain in a 007 movie. "For a young'un of your age and experience...? Well, now. I'd say a dollar an hour'd be more than fair to 'give' you, as you put it."

"Now Burnie, that ain't no decent living wage," Mr. Halsey said, putting his fingertips on my temples and turning my head back around so that he could finish. "What you really gonna pay this here boy?"

"'Living wage?'" Sykes mocked. "You sound like Ted Kennedy, sir. For young Timothy here, I offer a base pay of a dollar an hour, and at the end of the shift we'll see about a performance bonus, of an amount to be determined based upon my evaluation of the work in question."

"Well-sir, my grandbaby ain't got nothing else to do on this long afternoon—do you, punkin?" Grandy smiled and crinkled his warm, loving eyes.

"I'm not sure I want to work today," which made the men guffaw and stamp their feet.

The barber spun the chair around and looked at me, brandishing his snipping scissors. "Tim, the unfortunate reality is that you're likely to have to get up and go to work every day for the rest of your life, so I say, might as well get used to it. Isn't that so, boys?"

"If that ain't the god's truth," Rabbit said, "I don't know what is."

We stayed a while longer. The men all sat there, smoking and reading and jacking their jaws about this and that. I hoped by the time we left everyone would have forgotten this business about me going to work for Mr. Sykes.

But nobody forgot anything, and as we went to leave, Grandy told my new boss I'd be along soon as we were done with lunch. "Where you want him? The car lot?"

Mr. Sykes owned a number of businesses and properties. The mean old man narrowed his eyes at me. "Send him over yonder to Mayfield Acres instead."

Gulp. Mayfield Acres, despite its bucolic sounding name, was not a nice place.

CAREFUL AND CAUTIOUS like I'd been taught, I rode my bike down the side of Highway 79, then cut through a stand of longleaf pines and a couple of dirt roads. Mayfield Acres was a trailer park off River Road where what my folks called 'white trash' lived—poor people. Black people had their own trailer park, but it was on the other side of the river. The schools weren't segregated, but the rest of Edgewater County often still seemed that way—the black churches, the black juke-joints, the black grocery store.

I parked my bike and crept inside a little shack with peeling paint and a tin roof on which hung a weathered sign reading *FRONT OFFICE*. Inside I saw Mr. Sykes standing over a plump, sad-faced older teenage girl sitting at the desk. "What do you mean you already gave them their deposit back—have you *inspected* that unit?"

Sniffling and red-eyed as though about to boohoo, she croaked in a tiny, chastened voice, "But but but Mr. Sykes, they told me you'd done signed *off* on their trailer!"

"God durn your bubble-headed little butt." He turned to me. "Boy, you and your granddaddy got yourselves some good timing—come along with me, now."

He opened a closet and got out a bucket, a mop, some rags and a grungy, half-empty bottle of 409, pushing me out the door. Taking such strides with his long skinny legs that I could barely keep up, he led me through the trailer park.

What I saw:

Laundry hanging on lines, broken down cars, overweight women sitting on makeshift wooden porches, kids playing kickball in the dusty dirt, flies buzzing around trash cans, all the trees cut down, sleeping mutts flopped in the sandy earth. My grandparents' yard was an Eden of azaleas and flowers and majestic oaks, but this looked and felt to me like a prison camp. Maybe Mr. Pirkle had been more right than wrong with his Auschwitz aphorism, but at the time all I knew was that if work would make me free of Mayfield Acres, I wanted to get started. What an awful place. I supposed people lived where they were able.

I recognized one or two of the kids, waved to them. They didn't wave back, only stared at me walking around with Mr. Sykes.

We stopped in front of a not-bad trailer. The scrubby yellowed grass around it needed mowing, though. Was that it? Mowing this little plot? I could run a mower like nobody's business. It wouldn't even take me an hour.

But I wouldn't get off so easy: "Look here, boy: There was a bunch of no-good son of a bitches living in here who skipped out on me, and I need you to put this trailer looking shipshape so's I can set to renting it out again. Think you can handle that?"

I wasn't sure, but I nodded and said uh-huh. He pushed open the door. The inside looked dark and gloomy, a mysterious cave.

"Now, I don't reckon I need to explain how to clean—do I, boy?"

I shook my head.

"Get to it, then."

Once inside, my eyes adjusted to take in a disaster area—the tenants had left an overflowing trash can with a cloud of gnats and flies swarming all around, the carpets covered in dog hair and crumbs, and a kitchen sink and countertops speckled with mysterious green crud. The smell was a mix of rotting garbage, smelly feet, and a weird chemical odor mobile homes always seemed to have.

I stood in shock. My mother and grandmother both kept spotless houses. "Mr. Sykes, a dollar an hour's not—"

He held up a hand. "All right, all right, listen here: you clean this up right, and I'll give you *twenty* dollars. It won't take you all that long. Helluva a lot more than the minimum wage—which in your case is a standard I'm not legally obligated to uphold."

I hadn't a clue what he was talking about, but a double sawbuck sounded like real money. I didn't never *ever* have a whole twenty in my pocket, except maybe at birthday-money time, which this year would be while we were at Myrtle Beach —*hoo*, boy! "Twenty bucks? Really?"

"If you don't get going, you'll be getting diddly-squat."

I shook the bottle of 409 and sprayed a few weak clouds

of vapor onto the creeping crud in the sink. "I might need some more of this."

He grunted. "I'll send Janice out for provisions—Mr. Clean, some paper towels, bathroom foam and maybe some of those blue pucks for the toilet, too. And I'll bring back a shop vac. On a cleanup job like this, you always vacuum last, backing your way out the door," he pantomimed, "so as to leave the interior spotless and pristine and ready to show. Understand?"

"Yes, sir."

"Very good." And he was gone.

I DREW in a big-boy breath and set to work. I began with the fridge. The power had been off, so inside was a damp, horrid mess of decomposing food: vegetables rotting in the bin, a carton of sour milk two weeks out of date, a dozen eggs, a half-eaten ham sandwich turning fuzzy and green, ketchups, mustards, and a couple of brown pears that were soft and leaking fluid. I gagged and started chucking food into the garbage can; the carton of eggs bounced off and dropped onto the floor, breaking open.

I cussed. I sweated. I picked up the eggs and felt like crying.

After dragging the leaking, full trash bag outside I found a fresh one under the sink, scattering a colony of roach-bugs when I opened the cabinet. Twenty dollars or not, this so-called 'work' was degrading and sickening. I imagined all my friends—and Shelby—pointing and laughing at me for having gotten myself into this literal mess.

But Mr. Sykes, and Grandy, were counting on me to do a

good job. A grownup's job. I went to prop open the front door, tried to get some air moving.

Mr. Sykes came back in a few minutes with a vacuum cleaner, a jug of ammonia, and two double rolls of Brawny paper towels. I was pleased—as depicted in numerous daytime television commercials, this product was capable of soaking up entire messes all at once.

Glancing over the countertops and peeking into the avocado green fridge, he inspected my progress. "Not bad, m'boy, not bad at all. Got to get in the corners a little better, though. Take your squirt bottle and mix this ammonia half and half with water."

I did so, feeling lightheaded as fumes went straight up my nose. I swayed on my feet and thought I'd pass out, but I hid this condition from Mr. Sykes.

"Back in a bit," he said, tromping out onto the deck and down the steps.

I retched into the sink I'd just begun to get clean.

DRIPPING with a sheen of sweat that in the humid afternoon had nowhere to evaporate to, I quit the kitchen and started on the bathroom. The black crud around the toilet base caused me to swoon anew, but after soaking it with the cleaner, it mopped up pretty easily.

Janice showed up with more cleaning supplies and a couple of sandwiches and ice-cold Co-colas, the big bottles. "Mr. Sykes says for you to take you a break, sugar. And for-me-to-help-you *fin*-ish," she added in a resigned, mopey cadence, her lower lip protruding.

I washed my hands and arms. We stood outside in the hot sun drinking our fizzy pop and eating chicken salad made with too much goopy mayonnaise and big chunks of celery, which I hated but couldn't spit out, not in front of Janice.

She reached around and tugged at her short-shorts, which even by the fashion standards of the day seemed one size too small. "How bad is it?"

I tried to play it cool, but my words tumbled out in an awkward rush. "Not as bad as before Mr. Sykes put me—had me—get on it."

She seemed skeptical. "I'll be the judge of that."

We went back in and I set to mopping. Janice opened the fridge. "Foo-wee." She sprayed another dose of extra-strength cleaner inside.

Working alongside Janice made me feel like a grownup— she wasn't barking orders at me the way my Daddy would when I was raking the yard. We were peers, both being paid by Mr. Sykes.

Then, I fantasized that Janice and I were married, and how at some point we were going to do *other* things married people do, things I didn't fully understand but which caused a mysterious stirring inside me—Shelby Fordham's face had much the same effect. This sensation I sought to quell by thinking about how much I despised the folks who'd left behind this mess.

Janice was like a whirlwind, and in less than an hour we had it squared away but for vacuuming, which I started to do. I went to plug it in, but there wasn't any power.

"Dang," Janice said. "None of us thought of that, did we? Just gather all the cleaning stuff and lock the door behind you."

"Yes, ma'am."

She snorted and scoffed. "Don't you call me 'ma'am,' little boy. I ain't that much older than you."

I finished and trudged back up to the office with the mop

and rags and leftover paper towels. Janice met me outside and handed me an envelope, told me how much she enjoyed working with me, then laughed like it was some kind of joke.

An Iroc-Z driven by a thick-necked, high school football jock, who I supposed was her boyfriend, pulled into the dusty turnaround in front of the office. She got in without saying goodbye and they peeled out. At the last second, Janice winked and waved to me with her pretty painted nails. I fantasized that she wanted to be my girlfriend, but hadn't known how to break the ice.

I opened the envelope. Inside, I found money, and a note:

5 hours x 1 dollar/hr = 5.00
plus 20.00 bonus
Good job, boy

A bonus—and yet, I thought to myself, he hadn't come back to check on my work. In any case, the money in my hand felt like the fortune of a king.

Filthy and exhausted, I pedaled back to Grandy's. Greeting me on the front porch with two cold, sweating glasses of sweet tea adorned with sprigs of fresh mint, he asked me how my first day at work had been. Not about what I'd done, mind you, but rather how much I'd been given by old Burnie Sykes, who was the kind of skinflint, it was said, who probably still had the first dime he ever made.

"How's it feel to have your own money?"

I told my grandfather it felt good. And unlike Grandy, who'd been sent to Europe either to kill or be killed, if the worst thing that ever happened to me was getting a twenty in my hand after cleaning up some nasty person's mobile home, life would probably end up pretty darn sweet and easy.

"Don't just fritter it away, now—spend it on something that matters."

I would. I was going to call Shelby, maybe as soon as that night. *Saturday Night Fever* would only be playing at the Palmetto for a few more days; the summer of my almost-thirteenth year wouldn't last forever.

the night i prayed to elvis

LORD, BUT IT'S DUSTY OUT HERE BY THIS DURN road, another hot stupid boring old Monday. In the summer I can't hardly tell what day it is, except maybe by what Mama fixes for supper. She has her schedule—for example, Monday is pork chops—because Daddy's one of them that likes things to stay they way they are. He don't like surprises much. Says stuff coming out of nowhere, when bad things happen which you ain't ready for, that there's what makes life harder than it ought to be.

A bend in the road.

Our house sits up on a flat rise and is set so's you can look down the road both ways, but only a little because there's a curve one way going down into the woods and then another heading back to the main highway. Anything could come down the road from the highway, but from the other direction is only the river, and old men like my Daddy who fish in it.

On a dull as dishwater day like this I sometimes stand looking around that bend, picturing a bus coming around the corner, but not the school bus I sit on with my best friend

Darlynn Murtishaw. On the bus is where we talk about records we hear on *Kasey Casem's American Top 40* and who was on *American Bandstand* Saturday afternoon, and that takes us over to the schoolhouse. My imaginary bus doesn't go to the school—oh, no. Instead, my pretend bus is like the Partridge Family's bus, all colorful and happy, but on *this* bus are a different music group: the Beach Boys, all of them, coming to take me somewhere that's full of people and fun and songs.

And on this pretend bus, not only can we play the songs we like? But also we can play them as loud as we want?

Maybe the bus is set up so that we can all dance together too, and once we get to the beach there's going to be a concert and it's going to be for me. A bus ride to heaven, that's what it would be. Not for me alone, I reckon, but still mine.

When they come, I don't know if I'll ask them to go and stop by Darlynn's house to get her to come with us. She's eleven. It's hard to be best friends with someone who's eleven but when you're only ten. That's a big difference. This summer she got her boobies, wears brassieres. She acts too big for her britches. And the boys, now they stand in a line to talk to her.

On an August day like this, a body could do for some couch-sitting inside where it's cooler, but I don't want to lay around with Mama looking at the stories on TV—it makes me feel tired, and empty inside my head and heart. I'd rather play my records and dance, but I can't do that when someone's looking at TV. Tonight when I pray, I'm already going ahead and asking Santa Claus for those headphones like singers wear when they're making their records, which is what I will do someday since I like to sing so much. With some headphones I can keep my music to myself, keep it inside my head where it won't bother no one while they look at their TV shows.

The war with Daddy (and sometimes Mama) over my music makes me so mad I want to cuss. It's gotten so bad I sometimes spend all night listening to my little radio right next to my ear turned down real real low. It's the only time I can listen and not get my butt spanked over that "thump-thump-thumping mess on them records of your'n." Daddy's old, he don't know what's good and what's not.

When he's home and I'm playing my KC & the Sunshine Band album, which is one of the few whole albums I have, he gets extra ornery. "How long is that same durn song gonna go on?" That always makes me laugh at silly old Daddy: KC & the Sunshine band has a whole bunch of songs, and every one of them is good, but it's definitely not one long song. Nobody puts out a record that's one long song. That's just dumb.

"Turn it off," he finally begs me. "Lord, set me free."

P'shaw, I say.

Daddy might get his drawers in a bunch over the sound of my music, but Mama's always more worried about what they're saying, which I will admit is sometimes hard to understand, especially with the Bee Gees.

"What difference does it make what they're saying?"

"Because nowadays there ain't no telling what them people are singing about."

"Mama, whatever it is, it ain't nothing bad! They wouldn't play it on the radio if it was."

"That's why they make it so hard to understand—to trick you. Just like 'Louie, Louie.' I remember at your Daddy and me's prom night, the principal made them fellas quit playing when they started *that*."

Come to think of it, Mama's kind of right about that one

—I don't got no idea what they're saying in 'Louie, Louie.' But like I was trying to tell her, if it sounds good and you can dance to it, what difference do a bunch of stupid words make?

Neither of my parents mind when I play one of Mama's old Beach Boys records, which I didn't understand until she explained that those songs were the ones that she and Daddy liked when they were first getting together, before he went off to Vietnam. Maybe that's why I love the Beach Boys so much—I could hear that music when I was still inside her tummy. It makes me feel kind of special, what with Mama and Daddy and me all liking the same music. For once.

Mama says her favorite singer, though, is still Elvis, "like he was before he went off into the Army." I can't hardly believe they made Elvis go into the Army—wasn't what he did important enough that he could get out of it? That's all over my head. I reckon the reason is that he had to go and fight in Vietnam like Daddy did with his friends Ronnie Pettus and Buddy Sykes. Daddy and Buddy came home, but Ronnie didn't. Ronnie had been Daddy's best friend. That's about the long and short of what he's got to say about Vietnam—that he took and left his best friend behind, which for a long time I didn't understand meant that Ronnie got killed there, and not just left.

"I didn't get so much as a scratch, but Ronnie didn't make it past the second week in the field. Great god almighty," and then Daddy's eyes look all red and funny and he don't want to talk no more about Vietnam. I ought to ask him if they ever seen Elvis when they was overseas, but I reckon if Daddy had he would have told me that before now. Wouldn't he?

We was talking about Elvis not too long ago: Mama got all excited when she heard on the news that he was going to have a singing over in Columbia, at the big coliseum where we went to the circus that one time when I was little. She got so worked up that she decided we was going to go see him, and then, buster, I can tell you I got all excited, too.

Daddy said we couldn't afford it, though. After that Mama and Daddy had a knock-down drag-out like I ain't never seen.

"You're still just jealous of him like you used to be," Mama said.

Daddy replied that people like us don't run around and go to no concerts, and that she better forget about all that mess. Since Daddy butters our bread and all, what could Mama say? That was that.

All of a sudden Mama's standing out on the porch with her arms akimbo, which means that her stories must be done because that's when she comes looking to check on me. "Lucy-Loo, I swear to goodness but I'm not going to tell you again about playing in that nasty ditch."

"I'm not messing around in the ditch—I'm waiting for someone."

"*Who*? Timmy?" Timmy being my big brother.

"No one."

"Well then, which is it? Someone or no one?"

I might as well be out with it, but as soon as I open my mouth I feel silly and stupid. "The Beach Boys."

Mama snorts and folds her arms. "The Beach Boys."

"*Yes*," which I say like I'm real sure of myself and so what? I stick my chin out. "They're coming to pick me up and take me to their beach concert."

Mama gets a look on her face like she's about to both laugh and cry at the same time, the way her face gets when she sits at the table drinking tea, fanning flies and flipping through our baby pictures. "Is that what my little angel thinks? That the Beach Boys are just around that bend?"

I feel like a dumb little first grader. "*No.*"

Now she's got her regular old Mama face again, which around her eyes and mouth is kind of tired looking. "Lord have mercy but the stories you tell, young'un. Now get in the house and wash them hands and feet before you catch every disease in the book."

"Yes ma'am." I run barefoot up onto the porch. "Can I play my records till Daddy gets home? Please *please*," begging before she has a chance to answer.

"I reckon so. Not loud, now. Mama's head hurts."

"Yes ma'am!" I'm so excited that I can't even decide what song I want to hear first.

"Lord, but it's as hot as the devil's kitchen out here..." Mama's looking down the road at the bend like she's waiting on something, too: Daddy, I guess, who ought to be getting home from work before too long. "Let's go back inside, my littlest angel. If the Beach Boys is coming, I better go put my face on. After I get Daddy's pork chops breaded."

I go skip-skipping into my room and strike a pose with my pretend microphone: "Thank you, Edgewater County!" I blow kisses to my audience, spin around and flop down to flip through my singles. I like to mix them up, to make a stack of wax as Timmy calls it when you put a bunch of records on at once. The only one I know I don't want for sure is 'Nights on Broadway,' because I swear to goodness but I can't get that one out of my head. "I'm Your Boogie Man" and "You Make Me Feel Like Dancing" and "Dancing Queen" are ones I can't seem to get tired of no matter how hard I try, so I pick those and then "Whatcha Gonna Do?" and a couple of others.

And so now I'm the dancing queen in my little room, spinning and twirling and sneaking the volume knob up a little between each song until Mama hollers from in the kitchen for me to turn that racket down. She calls my music a racket, but sometimes I come out of my room and catch her swinging and bobbing a little bit in front of the stove or the sink.

Like right now. "*Wha-choo gonna do when she says goodbye; wha-choo gonna do when she is gone?*" and sure enough she's shaking her tail feather. But only a little. And only, I reckon, because she's by herself. It's weird how Mama and Daddy don't never listen to music except when we go to church, and I can tell you church music don't sound nothing like Pablo Cruise.

I dance my way into the kitchen and give Mama a start, making her jump. "*Lord have mercy*—Lucy, you liked to give me a coronary." She goes back to breading Daddy's pork chops, tossing one onto the cutting board in puffs of flour that go *poof* in little clouds.

"Sorry, Mama." I dance my way around the kitchen table, singing along. "But this is my favorite."

"Oh, you say that about every durn song. Go turn that down, now."

"You like this one, don't you, Mama?"

"I can't hardly understand a blessed thing they're saying."

Now the song's fading out. Mama's staring out the window, like her mind's a million miles away. "Don't stand out yonder by the side of the road waiting for somebody to come and get you."

I'm embarrassed again. My voice is so tiny that I can barely hear it over the air conditioner. "Mama—I know the Beach Boys ain't coming. It's pretend? Up in my head? Like a story."

"I understand that. But what I mean is that you can't sit on your butt waiting for everything in life to come your way.

Sometimes if you want something, you got to go on and get it... rather than waiting for it to come to you. You understand?"

I reckon I do. "Like when you want to go and get groceries from the store?"

"No. I'm trying to say to you that if you wait long enough in the same spot, you might get stuck there waiting and never..." She sighs like she's tired. "Nothing, Lucy. Your Mama's just running off at the mouth. I was not going to live my mother's life. Oh no. And I did not, not for a long time. But here I am. Mercy. Mercy. Here I am."

"Okay." I don't got a clue what she's going on about, but she's all distracted and standing there, looking at that pile of dusty pig meat waiting for the grease, and I'll be durn if she don't curse a little under her breath, rinse off her hands, and go back onto the porch smoking one of Daddy's cigarettes.

I run back into my room to find my record turning around and around, skipping right at the very end of the music when you can barely hear anything. I pick up the needle and pull it back, letting the next record fall.

Supper's good, but Daddy is a crab-cake, all grouchy and tired and hot. Timmy's not here tonight, and like I said, nothing burns Daddy up more than everyone not being at the supper table.

"Where's that boy of mine?"

"He's over at the Waugh's playing touch football and then taking supper with them," Mama says as she gets up to refill Daddy's sweet tea for him. "Or so he says."

"I'm going to whup that little cuss but good." Daddy smacks his lips like he tasted something bad. But he didn't—

after he cuts into his pork chops, which are so tender he only has to use his fork, he goes *Mm-mm*. "That boy's missing out on a fine meal his Mama spent all afternoon fixing. That ain't right."

I don't see what the big durn deal is. "Maybe he's tired of eating pork chops on Mondays."

"Do what?"

"I *said,* maybe he's tired—"

He drops his voice. "Now hush up, Lucy, before you hurt your mama's feelings." He gestures with his fork toward my plate, where I'm pushing peas around. "Eat like you appreciate what you got in front of you, now."

"Yes, sir."

Mama comes back with his tea, and then the rest of the meal is us sitting and eating with the sound of our forks and knives going *squeak* on the plates, and also the *squeak-squeak* of the window unit, of course. But right about the time Mama gets set back down good and picks up her fork, we hear this godawful racket from out on the back porch where the washer sits: *THUMPA-THUMPA-THUMPA*. It's off-balanced again, which happens all the time.

Mama fusses and scolds about needing a new machine.

Daddy drinks his tea and as he's swallowing, his big Adam's apple bobs up and down. "Maybe we'll run over to the Sears one day soon and take us a look. I sure can't see putting no more money into that thing," which is what Daddy said last year when he wanted a new truck. "It's about plumb wore out."

"*One day, one day soon*," Mama says in a voice like she's mocking Daddy. "It's always 'one day soon' with you."

Daddy pokes out his lips. "I'll have you know I resent that, Mother."

Mama looks like she bit into a persimmon or a sourball.

She gets up and shuffles through the kitchen toward the back porch, mumbling and grumbling.

"Sissy," he says. "Look here: You want to ride over to the Sears tomorrow?"

"To Columbia?" Once in a blue moon we ride over there, usually on Saturdays, but I can't ever remember going on a Tuesday. "*Tomorrow*?"

"You know what? Let's take your Mama appliance shopping tomorrow afternoon. I get off at three. If the delivery truck's early, maybe by two."

Oh my goodness gracious—and what else do they have at Sears besides washers and everything else under the sun? Records. Lots of them. I've been saving nickels and dimes all summer in a jar under my bed, I think I almost have enough to buy a whole album again. I got my KC and the Sunshine Band from Santa Claus last year, but if I have to wait until Christmas to get another album, I'm liable to bust.

I explode with excitement, yes yes yes to this idea, Daddy.

"Settle down now," he says. "I ain't never seen anyone get so excited by the notion of going washing machine-hunting. Must be because you ain't the one what's got to pay for it," which cracks him up like when Jerry Clower is on *Hee-Haw*.

When Mama comes back to the table and he says to her what we're going to do tomorrow, she doesn't get half as excited as me, even though she's the one who wants the washer in the first place: A question, but she don't put it like one. "Will wonders never cease," is all she says.

"All right now," Daddy says. "*In everything give thanks, for this is the will of God.*"

Now, Mama's in church every Wednesday night and twice on Sunday, but something about Daddy quoting the Bible sets her off. At first she don't say anything, but I can see on her face that she's ticked off. I think I understand why—most

Sunday mornings she's got to half drag him to church, because he'd rather sit outside on the porch and look at the paper.

Finally, she says, *"Unto thee, O God, do we give thanks, unto thee do we give thanks: for that thy name is near thy wondrous works declare."*

I swear to goodness but I think she's being all smartypants. She's looking right smack at Daddy instead of having her eyes closed or else looking up to the Lord in His heaven.

Daddy's chewing and smacking. "I tell y'all what—this here's some good eating, Mother. Bless your heart for everything you do."

I barely hear them—all I can see are about a hundred different album covers all spinning around in my mind, like when I run across one of them record club ads in Mama's magazines. I keep begging to let me get the six records for only a dollar (or sometimes a penny!) but Mama keeps insisting that it ain't nothing but some trick for getting a whole mess of money out of you sometime later. No matter what's to come tomorrow, the rest of my supper tastes extra good.

"Once Daddy gets home, you'd best be ready to go," Mama says from my doorway the next afternoon. She's gone and put on makeup, and also changed into going-to-town clothes, which fall somewhere between house clothes and church clothes—a decent and proper dress, but nothing fancy, sandals and no stockings. "We don't want to dawdle."

"We won't."

"All right now, young lady. I'm serious."

I don't know why she's worried—I never wanted to go nowhere more than I do that Sears. All I been thinking about all day is them records they got over yonder. "Yes ma'am. I just need to brush my hair and put my money in my pocketbook."

Daddy comes in and dumps his keys and change on the table, plops down heavy in his chair, kicks up the footrest and sighs. He has to go in to the grocery store real early on Tuesdays because that's when one of the big trucks comes. He's important—he's the produce man.

"I'm wore slap out." He goes on to roll his eyes and talk about *The Wheels* having been there today. You'd think he meant the big truck, but what he really means are the big wheels—the grocery store is one of them that's in every town, and *The Wheels* are the men from the district office. "Them puffed up jaybirds was looking cockeyed at everything today. Great god almighty. One of them took out a white glove and started running his finger every which way. Like we don't keep no clean store."

Mama, who hears this same speech every time *The Wheels* come around, squints hard-eyed and suspicious at Daddy. "Well—ain't we going?"

"Do what now? Going where?"

"Don't you want to get on over yonder before that five o'clock traffic hits?"

"Over *where*?"

"Lord help," Mama says. "I should've known."

Daddy picks up yesterday's *Edgewater Advocate* and fans himself. "Go *where* now?"

I can't help myself. My whole head is hot. "*To the Sears to get Mama a washing machine!*"

He rubs his temples like he's tired, but his eyes look all twinkly. "Oh, but I'm so tired my legs are tingling. We got in coconuts and pineapples today, girls. Big old crates of them. If y'all will let me nap for an hour or two…"

Mama's eyes roll back in her head like that epilectric girl at school. Her mouth is set in that upside down smile she gets when she's mad about something, but don't want to say what she's on about. But this time she up and does: "I knew you were all talk yesterday. Knew it just as sure as I'm standing here."

Daddy's got a funny little smile. He slams the footrest down and goes into the bedroom, shuffling his feet like the tiredest man in Edgewater County.

I feel like I'm going to cry. "Oh, let's just go on without him. Please?"

She scoffs and p'shaws. "I can't stand driving with that bunch of crazies over there."

"But Mama—"

"Besides, sugar, I can't go and buy nothing without Daddy."

"Why not?"

"You'll understand one day."

Right then Daddy comes busting back out of the bedroom, and ta-da, he's done changed out of his work clothes. I can smell that he's put on a fresh coat of his Old Spice. That old rascal.

He claps his hands together. "You got your checkbook, Mother? We're a-gonna need it."

Mama's mouth is hanging open like one of them crappie that Daddy and Grandy catch when they go fishing up by the dam. "You turd."

Now Mama and Daddy start laughing. She goes and gives him a little kiss; he squeezes her rump, which he only does when they are both happy.

I run to get my jar of change.

When I come back out Daddy's drinking himself a Fresca, which he likes better than them Co-colas and RC Colas which, he says, give him thick nasty spit at the back of his throat.

He asks Mama, "Where's my firstborn? I know he don't want to miss out on a ride over to the city."

Mama's fussing around getting her pocketbook together. "He took and rode over to the state park to go swimming."

"With who?"

"With that bunch he runs with."

Daddy looks all pinch-faced like Mama did when she thought we wasn't going to get the washer. "He'll probably have more fun doing that anyway, I reckon... all right now, let's get ourselves road-bound. It's a helluva," catching himself before Mama can say *You better hush that filthy mouth Travis Latham*, "heckuva drive all the way over yonder."

"Oh, fiddlesticks. It ain't but a half hour. You drove twice that far to go to Hartsville with Hill Hampton and look at the car auction, and we wasn't even looking to buy nothing."

"I was too," holding the door open for Mama. "I just didn't find nothing I liked."

"P'shaw." But not like when she's calling bullcrud on something—she's got a cutesy little smile and he does too, the both of them looking at each other direct into the eyes. "Now, can we go, please, Mr. Latham?"

"I don't see why not."

PULLING into the Sears parking lot there's a mess of other cars, which makes Daddy ask what in tarnation all these people are doing out shopping on a regular old Tuesday. Mama and Daddy both can't stand crowds and standing in line, not even at the Sideboard Steakhouse in Tillman Falls, but I think it's worth it cause they got one of them hot bars

The Night I Prayed to Elvis 73

now with macaroni and cheese and Swedish meatballs and cakes and pies. If Mama hadn't wanted a new washer so bad I reckon she wouldn't've wanted to come over here at all—the whole drive she sat with her shoulders up around her ears, holding onto the dashboard whenever a big truck blew past us.

Mama grew up out in the country, right where we live now. She says she didn't get very far in life, only down the road a piece from Grammy and Grandy's house. So maybe that's why she don't like the city much. I don't know that Daddy does either, and I reckon we could've gotten ourselves a washer over in Tillman Falls, but Daddy says there's deals to be had at a big store like Sears.

And what a big store this is! We go in through the sliding doors, *whoosh*, and then there's everything a body could ever want or need, if you got enough nickels and dimes and quarters.

I wish I could live in the Sears or the K-Mart—you'd never have to leave except maybe to run out to the grocery store, but them are never far away, sometimes in the same plaza as the other big stores. If I had all them records sitting there waiting for me to play them, I don't think I'd even remember to eat anyway. I could pick out pretty clothes right off the rack, lay on one of them new mattresses they got, get cold drinks out of the machine over in the little area that's near customer service, and then dance my way to the records and start flipping through until I find the one I want to play—a different one every night, as loud as I want. Loud enough to feel the words and the music in my bones.

Lucky for me the washers and dryers are right near the TVs and radios, which are right near the racks of records, so Mama says I can go over there by myself while they shop, which makes me so glad—normally she likes to keep me close at hand, but dang if I'm not almost a 6th grader at the middle school, and that makes me almost *this close* to being a teenager like Timmy. So, I go dilly-bopping my way down the rows of washers, past the stereo sets and the wall of TVs, a dancing queen in her castle.

A little knot of people are standing at the TVs, shuffling around with their arms folded. The TVs are all on the same channel, the sight of which always makes my head feel funny like that time when I was little and Mama took me and Timmy to the picture show in Tillman Falls to see *The Aristocats* and we sat way too close to the screen. And after a big closeup of Duchess, with her white fur and sparkling eyes, I got sick to my stomach and we didn't get to see the end of the movie. Dizzy, like.

People are *hubbub*-ing and shaking their heads. A woman dabs at her eyes. Her husband says to another man, "Well, this just beats all I ever heard."

The man, about my daddy's age, sucks his teeth and says, "It's like, dang. The King." He blinks his eyes and his cheeks get red and then he walks away fast.

A man with a Sears nametag on his short-sleeve plaid shirt says, "Well, this must be some kind of tragedy. A *tragedy*."

"Mister, why's Elvis on them TVs?"

The man who works there says, "They saying that he died, honey. I don't half believe it... but there it is."

"Elvis?" My stomach feels like it does when you go over the rolly-coaster at the State Fair. I can't hardly find my voice. "Do *what*?"

The woman breaks down sobbing now like Daddy does when we go out to the cemetery for him to see the gravestone of his friend who didn't come back from the war. He don't know that I know he cries like that because he makes me wait in the truck. Crying like that is something you're supposed to do by yourself, I reckon, which makes me scared to see this woman crying like she done started right here in the middle of the Sears.

Something snaps inside my head: *I got to go and get Mama.*

I run back past the stereos toward the washers. Mama is lifting up lids while Daddy and another man with a Sears name tag stand talking with their hands on their hips like Daddy done when he went to Hill Hampton Motors to get his truck last year. I start hollering at the top of my lungs to get their attention.

Mama turns white as one of our bedsheets. "Lucy, what's wrong?"

"Mama—*Elvis died.*"

Her eyes get all big, dart over toward the salesman. "Oh, sissy, now hush up with your stories. That's ugly to say about someone. Especially *Elvis.*"

"No," the Sears man says. "She's right. Heard it on the radio, right before I walked over to help y'all."

"Elvis *Presley?*" Daddy says, like there could be anybody else in the world named Elvis.

"Hell of a thing," the salesman says. "Heck, I mean."

Mama's got a funny look on her face like the time the man come to tell us how much it was going to be to put a new roof on the house. "Where'd y'all hear that mess?"

I grab her by the hand, hustle her over to the TVs. Mama's hand in mine is clammy and cold. We stand there looking at the 5 o'clock news, which ain't even about Elvis no more. "Lucy you'd best quit messing around with me today," and she says it all mad but I swear to her that I ain't messing with anybody.

The other Sears man is still standing there in his short sleeved shirt and tie and name tag. "Help y'all with anything?"

She asks him about Elvis. He shakes his head sadly. Mama about keels over.

"Watch yourself, ma'am." The Sears man takes her by the elbow and leads her over to a Lay-Z-Boy they got sitting in front of the TVs, so's you can see how it feels to sit and look at them, I reckon.

"What happened? Did he get killed in a car wreck?"

The man tells us that they don't know yet, but that it might be a heart attack or stroke. And then he goes off to talk to a man fiddling around with a console TV, one that has a stereo built inside.

"Mama—I can't believe it," with my voice all shaky.

"I still *don't* believe it."

"*But it was on the TV earlier.*"

"I know, Sissy. I believe you. Here," pulling herself back up like when she's real creaky and tired and still has the kitchen to clean up. "Let's go look at your records."

The crying woman from earlier is on the record aisle. She looks half crazy, her eyes all red and wide. Her husband has a stack of albums in his arms. "They don't got poop for Elvis records in this damn store," she says, her voice all harsh and angry.

Oh no. I had decided to get an Elvis album! I have that feeling like when I caught my cousin from North Carolina stealing money out Mama's pocketbook that one Thanksgiving—like something personal has been done to me and me alone. The plastic separator that says *ELVIS* is flat against the one in front of it that says *ELO* which is for Electric Light Orchestra. "Mama, she done took every one."

"You're damn right," the woman says with a mean cut on her voice. She makes a *HAH* sound and then drags her husband off, hurrying on toward the checkout stand with her stolen Elvis records. "These is gonna be worth a lot of money now."

Mama goes right over to where they're standing and starts flipping through the records. She cuts her eyes at the woman's back, but they've down hightailed on their thieving way.

Mama looks mad enough to bite a rock in half. "Well, I'll be *shit*. That painted-up hussy took every last one."

I ain't never heard my Mama use a bad word like that. Now I feel like I'm about to cry. And I do—I start blubbering, sucking breath. "Mama, I can't believe that Elvis is dead."

"Well, darling." She pulls me to her. "Just pick you out something else you want and Daddy'll get it for you."

"Okay," sniffling. "I reckon."

Mama lets me go and wanders off, hugging herself like she's cold.

I can't hardly think straight now. All I can think about is Elvis and the fact that that crazywoman took all his records. I start flipping through looking but I can't find nothing I want. Not until I find something special that's stuck in the wrong place, something that makes me catch my breath like I seen a ghost:

Elvis—there he is, in a shiny gold suit. A big picture and then a bunch of little ones, the same one, repeated all over the white album cover. *50 Million Elvis Fans Can't Be Wrong*. I get chicken skin over my whole body.

"*Mama*." My voice screeches and my throat hurts. "Come back quick!"

I start going toward the washers, but both Mama and Daddy are already running my way.

Daddy looks scared. "Sissy, now what is it...?"

"Look look *look*."

Mama's scared face melts away when she sees the record. "Oh, Daddy. Look at that."

He takes the album out of my hand, says to Mama, "You used to have this one, didn't you, honey?"

"I did." Mama takes the album and holds the cardboard cover to her body. "I don't know what happened to that thing."

"I think we threw it out that time when Timmy was a squirt and took a screwdriver to all them records that used to sit under the coffee table... here: let me buy it for you."

"Oh," Mama says, her mouth downturned. "We don't need to buy some stupid old record."

"P'shaw," Daddy says, taking Mama's favorite word right out of her mouth and making it his own. "And you, pudding-pie, go and get yourself one too."

"But Daddy, they ain't no more Elvis records but that one."

"Well, go get something else. Get some of your music. Besides, I ain't never seen you play a Elvis record in your life."

"But he's *dead*. I shouldn't buy no one else's record. Not today."

"That don't matter. Go on, now. It's not every day we get over to the high and mighty Sears."

"Yes, sir." And I kind of forget about Elvis for a minute. Not for long. But I reckon Daddy's right. I didn't never care for Elvis much before right now.

As I run back to the records, I hear Daddy say to Mama, "I don't think they's too many good deals here. Let's just run over to Mr. Vincent's tomorrow or the next day. Keep our money in Edgewater County." If Mama's got anything cross to say about not getting her washer, I don't hear her. I look back to see them hugging, and it looks like Mama is crying, finally, which makes me feel bad for her.

I flip through the albums until I feel like I'm going crazy.

Everybody's buying that Fleetwood Mac thing but I don't like it that much, leastways not what I keep hearing on the radio? And I don't like the picture of them two people on the cover, something about it seems weird? Andy Gibb, now, I love that one song of his they been playing all summer, so I bet all the other ones he has are good too, and so I pick that one.

Andy Gibb's album cover is perfect: ain't nothing weird about a picture of somebody who's that handsome. He looks like a dream, an angel with his white teeth and tan skin and shiny hair.

Daddy buys the records and we go home, riding in silence but for Paul Harvey on the radio, talking about Elvis.

When we get home, Daddy yells at Timmy for having his music too loud, Mama goes in and puts on the TV and looks at the national news, which is all about Elvis, and she dabs her eyes all the way through eating the supper we brung home from the Burger Chef out on the highway. We sit there eating and not talking about nothing, which is how Daddy usually wants it.

Timmy spoke up with that smart-alecky voice he always uses since he turned into a teenager. "Elvis looked all fat and sweaty in them pictures they showed of him when he came to Columbia."

"Timmy," Daddy said, putting his fork down. "Hush that smart mouth. Before I hush it for you."

"What?" Timmy says. "He did too look fat."

"We don't speak ill of the dead, son."

I GO BRUSH my teeth and get ready to say my prayers. It don't feel right doing it, but when I pray, I'm praying to Elvis, who has now gone home to his father's many mansions in the sky:

"Elvis: I know you are trying out your angel wings right now, but I want to pray that if you could, could you please ask Jesus to make my Mama feel better. I think she misses you something awful. I can't half believe you are gone, but if they say on the TV that you are, then I reckon you are. I'm sorry. Amen."

I feel naughty somehow, but not silly like when I'm wishing for the Beach Boys to come around the bend to get me. Elvis can hear me now, unlike the Beach Boys, so that makes it not silly at all, not so long as Jesus don't mind that I talked to Elvis instead of him tonight.

As everyone else toddles off to bed, the house gets quiet. Mama came by earlier and stuck her head in saying goodnight. I didn't say anything back—I laid here pretending I was already asleep. I don't know why I did, other than the fact that I keep feeling sad and lonesome.

Maybe I'm sad because summer's almost over. Before you know it, school will start and next the State Fair will going on and then Thanksgiving and then Christmas will come, and then the New Year, which, come to think of it, is another time Mama always acts sad. Last year when we was watching the ball drop on TV—it's the one night I get to stay up as late as I want because she always says there's only one New Year's Eve a year, and in its own way it's as special a day as Christmas or Easter—Mama said to me that if you take a notion, New Year's is a time when you can start over and fix whatever didn't go right in the old year.

I sure didn't know that Elvis was going to die this year, but as far as I can tell, dying is something that nobody can fix. But I reckon he didn't expect to either. No one ever does; when you die, I reckon it just kind of happens, like with my grandmama a few years ago. But that's a long way off for me. Ain't no need to worry about going to heaven, not when you are ten years old and about to start the 6th grade.

spin the bubble

THE CRUSH I SUFFERED OVER COLETTE CARROLTON, oh, roundabout eighth grade: a monster, a ruthless emotional obsession which threatened to consume my consciousness. Like the melody of a catchy pop tune, her alliterative and lyrical name stuck in my head—Colette Carrolton, Colette Carrolton, Colette Carrolton; she came to me as a song. The adolescent lust for her gripping my intellect and nether region —I mistook the sensation for love—seemed indefatigable.

Interminable.

Impossible.

More than lust, or as-much-as, was the simple fact that I liked her. We got along. Mostly. Like friends, almost.

Perhaps less than I fantasized.

I was a dreamer, yes, but one with a strong streak of realism. I understood I didn't have a chance—my folks didn't belong to the country club like hers, for one big reason. I wasn't pug-ugly, but presenting as neither athlete nor scholar nor quick-witted charmer, I also suffered from an advanced case of lingering, tenacious baby-fat, as well as a Jackson Pollackesque splatter of freckles on my face that'd landed me the unfortunate nickname 'Opie.' I had about as much chance of bagging Colette as I did Farrah Fawcett.

But then, a miracle: Between Christmas break and Easter week, I grew an astounding three inches. Now I'd become as tall as Billy Timmons, the tallest kid in homeroom. Billy'd had hair under his arms and a big Adam's apple since the middle of sixth grade. At last, I had caught up.

"Opie, you look like a different person," my friend Barrett said in gym class one morning. "Now if we could do something about that speckled mug of yours..."

"You're the one with the zits." The remark was below the belt, I know—Barrett's own ascent into puberty had produced an outbreak of virulent, scaly pustules. "Crater face."

"Zits, they'll go away eventually. But you? You'll always be a freckle-faced dork."

Touché. But, freckles aside, I now felt like a different me, more confident—ascendant, even, at the thought of high school next year.

Newfound confidence aside, by then I'd gotten over—or forced myself to get over—the lovely Colette, who'd started 'going with' Greg Rinker anyway. Rinker wasn't a smart kid, but from a well-off family and always wearing the hippest clothes and with feathered hair and a gold chain. Greg, always strutting around like Travolta in the opening credits of *Saturday Night Fever*. When he opened his mouth, he sounded like a complete dork, but I guess looks go a long way toward making up for a flaw like that.

So, of course I lost her to Greg Rinker. But then, you can't lose what you never had.

Oh! Colette was perfection. What was she doing with that chump? Occasionally I'd watch them holding hands or committing some other PDA—Public Display of Affection—

which of course was frowned upon not only by teacher and administrator alike, but in that context also by this heartsick narrator. Grim, facing up to this harsh reality every morning in home room.

BEFORE LONG, however, I began to receive my own first interest from a member of the opposite sex: Margaret Tuggle, a country mouse from across the tracks in Chilton, one of the 'river rats' as those citizens of Edgewater County were considered by the ever class-conscious Tillman Falls socialites, they of the Carolina horse country and revolutionary war monuments and the photogenic, historic town green. Margaret: A gawky, toothy, bespectacled mess, this young woman.

But... another miracle! Over the course of the eighth grade, the bookish, birdlike Ms. Tuggle also had her own amazing transformation—the frizzy hair became straight, the Coke-bottle eyeglasses were traded in for contacts, and a frumpy, hand-me-down wardrobe transformed into tight jeans and formfitting T-shirts. Margaret had become a regular cutie-patootie. Margaret and Tim-*slash*-Opie: both of us were now the Mark II models.

"Hi, Opie," she said one day in the breezeway. "What's doin'?"

"C'mon," I said. "Nobody calls me that anymore."

"I heard Gerald call you that just yesterday."

Cheeks aflame. "He's a big jerk. Let's make it Timmy, okay?"

"I'll call you whatever you want me to."

I ran into Margaret later that week at an afternoon matinee of *Star Wars*—the ninth of ten times that I saw the picture in the summer of 77 and spring of 78, back when big hit movies kept playing and playing, not long before the advent of home video would forever undermine such phenomena—and we ended up sitting elbow to elbow. About the time of the cantina scene I noted how she'd placed her hand on the arm of the seat next to mine—strategically—but I made no move.

But, why didn't I?

In a word, myopia: At that age, the approval of peers outstripped even the biological urges that, in moments private and public alike, gripped my mind. All I could see was the old ugly duckling Margaret, not the new model. If we were suddenly 'together,' I worried what my friends would say.

To wit, the next day at school: Gerald said he'd seen me coming out of the movie with Margaret. "You and that bucktoothed nightmare going together now?"

Defensive, I disproved the allegation in a manner most insulting to poor Margaret. "Wouldn't get near that thing."

"Me, neither," Barrett added. "Though she looks a helluva lot better than she used to."

Downplaying. "Yeah. She sorta does."

After a while, lovestruck Margaret—as I had cooled to her, she'd only gotten warmer—finally gave up. I didn't feel bad about my lack of reciprocation, not until later, when around the same time as Billy Timmons's party she started going with someone—a high school guy. A felt a tug—I didn't know it then, but this was regret whispering around my intellect and heart.

But never mind Margaret, for an incident occurred at Billy's party that, for an ephemeral moment, seemed to change everything.

One Saturday in May near the end of the term, Billy's folks let him have a bunch of us over in party in their newly renovated basement rec room, which had a pool table and a foosball table and a bar with a real beer tap, but of course Billy's dad made sure to remove the keg before we all got there. Mr. Timmons was an engineer over at the nuclear plant near the Sugeree River. The Timmons's, as a family, appeared to be doing quite well indeed.

My folks—well, my mom, anyway—expressed reluctance at my desire to attend this youthful celebration of our incipient, summertime freedom from scholarly constraints. Her sister Patty had gone off to a similar party when she was my age, and after word got to my grandmother that certain partygoers had been caught in the act of playing games like Seven Minutes in Heaven and Spin the Bubble, my aunt had gotten into serious hot water.

What's that? Yes, *yes*—I know it's really Spin the Bottle, but I was only ten back when I heard tell of that ancient family drama. Later, when I found out what the game was really called, I felt stupid, but in the time since had had trouble banishing the mistake from my mind.

As Mom cleaned up the dinner dishes in the kitchen on Friday night before Billy's party, I complained and begged. "But everybody's going."

"Would you jump off a bridge if everyone else did?"

Mom's cliché made me roll my eyes, even in 1977. "It's just a party."

She folded her arms. A dish towel, one with a Christmas motif that she nevertheless used all year round, hung off one forearm. "As long as Billy's parents are home, I reckon it'd be fine. Home by ten o'clock, though, and not a durn moment later."

On his way to bowling league, my father dropped me off at the Timmons's, on Pine Needle Way in one of the newer subdivisions. I was already feeling humiliated, as Mom had insisted on sending a tray of cupcakes with sprinkles on top, like something you'd serve at a six year-old's birthday party.

Mrs. Timmons, however, appeared delighted. None of the other kids' mom's had sent diddly-squat, she said. "Bless your mother's heart for such thoughtfulness," she said.

Barrett and Gerald greeted me; I was disappointed that Margaret, for whom I'd begun to feel not so much attraction as remorse, wasn't in attendance. Every time I saw her around town now with her new, ninth-grade paramour, Margaret looked prettier and prettier, and I felt like more of a dimwit. Shopping with my dad at the Sears outlet a Saturday or two ago, I ran into her and her mom. While I said *hey*, my erstwhile, potential girlfriend responded cold as ice, like the Foreigner song.

But the party was fun anyway: The music loud—"*Do you feel like we do?*" asked Peter Frampton; *wah-wah-wah* came the reply—the lights low, and the snacks tasty. Especially, I had to admit, Mom's cupcakes. Considering what happened later, I don't remember too many other details before the game of Spin the Bottle started, only that Colette seemed extra happy, and Greg Rinker...? Well, I noted that Greg had been sitting by himself the whole time in the corner, looking morose.

"What's going on with Rinky-dink?" As I chatted it up with Missy Johnston, another cutie, I leaned against the foosball table and tried to seem nonchalant. "Looks like he lost a bet."

"You didn't hear?" Missy said with a conspiratorial air.

"Supposedly he wanted to go all the way? But she didn't? And, like, now they're *finished?*" She motioned with her hands like an umpire calling an out. Missy seemed to glow at spreading this salacious gossip. "Can you believe it?"

"No kidding. Huh." My mind raced with newfound possibilities. "That brute."

"Oh my god, *I know.*"

As if on some cosmic cue Billy appeared carrying an empty Coke bottle, one of the big, heavy glass ones they sell in wooden crates.

"Ladies and gentleman," he announced with a lascivious leer, "may I suggest a few party games?"

My heart pounded as we gathered in a circle, all but Greg and a couple who had already, shall we say, embarked upon a game of their own making: Jenny Sennsen and my boy Gerald were in a shadowy, tangled knot on a sofa, oblivious to all but themselves. Maybe fifteen of us gathered in the circle, with none other than Colette directly across from me.

She smiled. Hot-cold sweat popped out on my forehead. I returned a grimace I hoped seemed friendly.

The game commenced. Billy, being the host, took privileges and spun first. The bottle turned fast before slowing to a stop; it pointed at me.

Billy leaned over and puckered up: "Oh, Opie, how I've longed for this moment."

I played along: "Never, Billy—not after the way you broke my heart with Barrett," who flipped me off. Everyone laughed, but I was still flushed with embarrassment and self-consciousness, like a virulent disease ravaging my insides.

Billy spun again, this time hitting the jackpot with Missy. They got up and stood in the middle. They regarded one another, both looking mischievous. In a flash, they seemed to grapple and begin kissing. Watching them with their tongues spinning around, I realized I was green, as green as could be regarding such matters, and now sat terrified at what was ostensibly expected of the participants in this erotic game. I glanced around at the various women, most of whom I'd lusted after but never truly imagined I'd be kissing like that. Colette being one of them.

Would it all be this easy? My heart pounded.

Spin, spin, spin; couples came together, some with enthusiasm, others less so. No one was willing to look like a coward, though.

The game went on until it was Colette's turn. She grasped the bottle and gave it a good spin; for whatever reason, she was looking right at me when she did so.

The bottle came to rest; for the second time, it pointed toward me.

My temples throbbed. Reality slowed down. I thought I would faint.

To the hooting and catcalls of the assembled partygoers, we both rose and stepped into the middle. I hesitated, until she took my hand and pulled me to her.

When we finally came apart with a smack, her cheeks were as flushed as mine felt. I tried to smile, breathless; she moved away with a sly wink. I felt dizzy—I had just been French-kissing the woman of my dreams.

I sat back down with a thud. She whispered something to Sarah Jamison, who hated me. Sarah scowled and made the gag-me motion with an index finger; Colette shoved at her playfully and shot me another quick glance, a secret smile. Sarah was always scowling, so I didn't pay her much attention.

I needed to calm down, so as the bottle was spun again, I got up and went to get punch. With a bit of a start I realized that Greg Rinker sat staring at me from his melancholy corner, seeing red. I averted my eyes—I didn't feel like having my first kiss, and first real fight, all in the same night.

The party screeched to a halt—Billy's mom came in and flipped on the light, asking a question to which she already knew the answer: "What on God's green earth do y'all think you're doing there with that bottle?"

Billy tried to explain, making up some cockamamie story. His mom dressed him down in front of us like a drill sergeant hectoring a hapless recruit. I felt for him.

Some kids who lived close by left; others, like me, made our calls to be picked up. On the way outside, I shared one more quick smile with Colette. Her eyes seemed to be saying 'yes, yes.' I swooned at my good fortune. I waved happily as she got into her dad's Mercedes, and drove away. It was so dark I couldn't actually see, but I imagined her looking back to me and yearning the way I did for her.

The next day, Sunday, took forever to pass. I started numerous times to call Colette, but kept chickening out. I didn't know what to say, but I also didn't want to go back to school on Monday without having made some effort to comprehend where things stood. The thought of calling her made me feel as though I'd swallowed a rock, and I ended up making no move to do so.

I tossed all night, finally getting up before dawn. I showered, scrubbing myself from head to toe; I spent many minutes combing my hair, and picking out a nice shirt and pants. Today it would be me as Tony Manero, not Greg, strutting down the school breezeway.

Met in the kitchen by my incredulous father, an early riser who normally had to coax his sleepyhead son out of bed, he mocked my early appearance. "Fancy seeing you at this tender hour. Have a bad dream?"

"Nah, just ready to get on over to school."

"Well, glory be. Today the devil's gonna need him a pair of ice skates."

I didn't care anything about any devils, only a special angel...

Homeroom lasted longer than a boring church sermon, with me watching the back of Colette's head the whole time—she'd come in late, and hadn't given me so much as a second glance before sliding into her desk and chatting with Sarah.

When the bell finally rang, I walked outside into the breezeway, my throat dry and my mind racing with the various permutations of what I'd say to Colette. I forced myself to be courageous; I recalled the euphoric intensity of the kiss. Obviously, she wanted me. No problem. I waited and watched everyone filing out.

Imagine, then, the shattering nature of the cold realization as I saw her, radiant, coming out of Mrs. Calhoun's classroom... and then walking straight over to that beady-eyed rat Greg Rinky-dink, who I hadn't even noticed leaning against the yellow lockers with his thumbs hooked into his belt loops. They both looked around before exchanging a quick, dry kiss.

A cartoon exclamation point appeared over my head—they were back together!

My bubble, burst.

Time passed, however, and I got over the pain: I started going with Missy, whose kisses were even better than Colette's, then Jenn Sennsen long after she and Gerald cooled off, and a couple others throughout high school, all 'real nice girls' as a nostalgic pop song puts it. I realize now I did a lot of wishing for girls to like me, and once it started, it's never seemed to stop. Maybe I'm lucky. Maybe I'm just a nice guy. You'd have to ask my wife.

Colette and Greg broke up at least two more times; they both dated other people, then were together again as juniors —she as prom queen, him in line as captain of the basketball team. As casual acquaintances, Colette and I chatted often; the kiss, having happened in eighth grade—a thousand centuries before—never came up again, nor, as I said, would it be repeated. After we graduated in '83, I lost touch not only with her, but with most all my childhood friends.

Decades passed as they will, until here I am back home, attending the twenty-year reunion of my high school graduating class.

Stunned and amazed, I marvel at how much people have changed; at how many faces and names became hazy and indistinct; a torrent of memories warm and otherwise are shaken a-loose, pieces of a past-puzzle dancing in my mind like snowflakes.

After a few G&T's I screw up the courage to go and tell Margaret Tuggle a big secret: how much I still regret turning down her adolescent entreaties of romance.

Recently divorced, Margaret, who's aged gracefully, becomes misty-eyed and gives me a drunken, sloppy kiss which annoys Becca to no end.

"That cougar'd better watch herself," she says, taking my hand. "This spot is taken."

"Just sentiment." This is said in legitimate reassurance—

we've been together a long time now, with Margaret but a childhood memory. "And a few too many martinis."

"Yeah, well," Becca says, pulling me close, "I've got a keeper. That I intend to keep." Which makes me happier than I could have imagined as a lonely country boy looking for love in all the wrong faces.

As for Colette Carrolton, she never appears at the reunion, nor does Greg Rinker. The interesting part? It's halfway through the evening before I even realize. A shame. It's fine. This not-so-youthful dreamer only wished to see if the dream girl has remained as beautiful, as young, and as perfect as he remembers her.

heroes and villains

THE COMICS CABAL, AS WE THOUGHT OF OURSELVES —Gerald Gorinsky, Barrett O'Steen, and me—became, over time, less about collecting than the act of creation. We were experts; we knew what we liked. We said: we, too, can do this type of work. Though we didn't yet have the term for it we'd gone DIY, and at Tillman Falls Middle School, this creative activity made us stand out—for one shining season, we were the media sensations of our eighth grade class.

I wasn't much of an artist, but as an aspiring writer, I could apply my burgeoning skill set to the crafting of narratives that Gerald and Barrett would later bring to vibrant, penciled and inked life. For his twelfth birthday, Gerald had gotten a learn-to-draw set, and learn to draw, by God, was what he'd done. Talent had struck.

By Easter break, we were up to our fourth issue. I was struggling through a fresh narrative arc for our resident hero, The Fox, a valiant warrior for justice. Our protagonist possessed the sensitive hearing and sharp eyesight of said animal, as well as superhuman strength, as is expected of such characters. He wore a suit like The Spirit, had a fox-mask designed to present a fierce, intimidating countenance. How he got this way we hadn't yet explained. But what were origin issues for, after all? All in good time.

The Fox's nemesis, The Cudgel, was Barrett's contribution: A monstrous mutant with glowing eyes and fists like hammers, The Cudgel broke into bank vaults and caused all manner of destructive mayhem. Rather than defeat him using brute force, in each story so far the physically outmatched Fox used his heightened senses and superior intellect to trick the villain. Our formula, repeated thrice, had earned us eager fans who awaited each new installment.

Our audience included the art teacher, Mrs. Daetwyler. Suitably impressed with our efforts, she allowed us the use of her classroom to work on the comics during free period. "If this were high school," she said, "I'd be recommending you young men for independent study credit." She flipped through the last issue. "Are you planning to add color? Margaret Tuggle is a very skilled watercolorist, you know."

"We like it black and white," Gerald said.

"Just something to think about."

"Do you like the stories?" I asked.

She smiled. "Very interesting—for a comic book, of course."

The teacher's use of the word 'interesting' rung in my head like an insult—a challenge, to present a greater depth of theme and dimensionality of character. It was clear that Mrs. Daetwyler regarded my storytelling as subservient to the more obvious skill employed in bringing the images to life, so this meant Gerald reigned as her star pupil. Admittedly, his panels came to fruition rich with depth and detail, with Barrett's inking also displaying a steady artistic hand, one much more apparent, I guessed, than the foundational contribution I made.

After Mrs. Daetwyler left us alone, we spitballed the upcoming issue. I proposed that we do a flashback origin story not for our protagonist, but The Cudgel: a dark tale wherein we discover he'd once been a good person, but the toxic waste accident that transformed his body also warped his mind; bitterness and anger over his misfortune had pushed him to a life of amoral, criminal mischief.

Gerald seemed indifferent. "Who cares about all that?"

"Well, see, then there's a reason—that he's not just bad for the sake of being bad."

"What's wrong with being bad-bad?"

"It's cool to know the 'why' of things," quoting Mr. Bingham, the social studies teacher.

"Bor-*ring*," Gerald said. "People want to see them fight, and for The Fox to outwit him. End of story."

I turned to the third member of our creative triumvirate. "What do you think?"

Barrett, scouring a tabloid comic collector's magazine for gems and rarities in the range of his modest, allowance-fueled budget, shrugged and yawned. "Whatever you guys decide is fine with me. But I do think we ought to start charging people a quarter to read, fifty cents to get a keeper-copy."

"Good idea." Gerald turned and gave me a smirk. "So that's two votes to one. No Cudgel origin issue."

I felt enervated and annoyed. My cheeks burned. I didn't have another idea.

Just then the unattainable object of my eye, the luminous and intelligent Colette Carrolton, sauntered by outside the classroom door alongside the skilled Margaret Tuggle. I wrenched my attention back to the matter at hand, though not without a struggle. "What if The Cudgel were finally put into a prison secure enough to hold him, and then The Fox, without a new challenge, must face up to some sort of real-life dilemma like... girlfriend stuff."

Barrett perked up, snapped his fingers. "The Fox could have relationship problems, like Spiderman."

I steeled myself. "And I also like the idea of Margaret," thinking *maybe Colette's a good watercolorist as well*, "adding color."

Gerald, looking at me as though I'd suggested he cut off his drawing hand, ignored my comment about Margaret. "Why don't we just come up with a new villain? The Fox needs a rogue's gallery. I'm sick of drawing The Cudgel anyway."

I wracked my brain. I'd already suggested one new antagonist—Onionskin Pete, a monster with a translucent epidermis and a bad attitude. Gerald had deemed OP too difficult to draw repeatedly.

I was out of ideas.

Then, inspiration: I'd begun to read regular books along with our beloved comics—Ian Fleming 007 adventures and science fiction like *Dune* and *The Stars My Destination*, both of which had blown my mind. "Okay okay," I said in a rush of inspiration. "An alien-villain. *The Thing From Another World* type of, well, thing. But more intelligent."

Gerald sighed and doodled. "But then we'd have to *explain* too much. Where the alien came from. What it wanted. Dialogue bubbles cluttering up my frames."

Barrett, on the other hand, became excited. "We could we could we could make it so that the alien wanted to help mankind? But was just, like, misunderstood? The Fox could kill it and in its dying breath it could say, wait wait wait but I came here to warn you about about about this this *comet* or *asteroid* that's coming to destroy the earth."

"Or," I suggested, "to maybe save us from ourselves, like getting rid of atomic bombs." I looked at my arm: chicken-skin. A good idea.

But this idea rendered Barrett, a movie geek—after *Star Wars*, who wasn't?—now only cautiously enthusiastic. "Eh. That's *The Day The Earth Stood Still*. Been done. But still—not a bad idea."

Gerald, whining and skeptical: "But then how will The Fox stop a comet from hitting the planet? He's not Superman."

I leaned back, looking up to the classroom ceiling. "Well... as a dying gesture of goodwill, the alien could give him new powers, maybe. Or... The Fox learns how to work the alien's spaceship, and at the last second blasts the comet out of the sky. Crowd goes wild."

Gerald clung to notions of familiarity and consistency. "I'd make the alien be a bad-ass and destroy stuff like The Cudgel. Then, The Fox tricks it and puts the creature into prison where scientists could study it."

Barrett, pleased: "There you go. I think we're getting off the track with all that comet stuff."

Gerald turned to me. "I want to see the story roughed out by Wednesday. I'll start working on the design of the alien." He got up to leave. "See you guys tomorrow."

After the door closed behind him, I mumbled, "I'm not sure you guys even need me anymore."

Barrett canted his head, frowned. "Don't be a brat. You can't always be the one."

"But I'm the writer!"

"You think Stan Lee doesn't oversee all the storylines? Gerald's our Stan Lee."

"I thought he was our Jack Kirby."

"Whatever. He's the leader."

Though I indeed looked up to Gerald, I'd considered our comics cabal to be more egalitarian in nature... but Barrett was right. Gerald had the talent, the power to make real our imaginative dreams. And the two of them obviously had plenty of their own ideas for stories. Not good ones, I thought. But like Barrett said: whatever.

I considered my next words, and wondered if I was about to make a mistake. But then, I had baseball season coming up, and then of course there were girls like Colette Carrolton about which to be concerned. Comics? Comics were kid's stuff. I'd show them who was in charge of his own destiny.

I took a deep breath. "I'm out," I said. "Tell Gerald he can write his own stories."

Barrett rolled his eyes. "You big baby. Suit yourself."

After school I walked out into the sunshine. Birds sang and bees buzzed around the brilliant blossoms of the azaleas planted at the front entrance to the school. I didn't feel sad, only that I had one less obligation. I pictured Gerald's face once Barrett told him the bad news. They needed me more than they understood. They'd come around, beg me to come back.

As I pedaled my Schwinn ten-speed out of the schoolyard, I shouted a greeting to Margaret and Colette, who were walking home.

They both smiled and waved. Margaret yelled, "Can't wait to see the next issue!"

That night, Gerald called me cussing up a storm. "You can't quit."

"Yes, I can."

"You think we need you? You're wrong."

I told him to go to hell, hung up, threw my history textbook across the room.

Later, I felt regret. But after he was so nasty, I swore I'd never work with my friend again.

In the end, I was validated: without me, Gerald and Barrett never finished another issue of The Fox. In their defense, though, both had experienced extenuating circumstances—Gerald got sick with strep throat and missed a week of school; in the meantime Barrett started going with Angela Fortescue, a blonde cutie who'd moved to Tillman Falls earlier in the year. And, like I said, I had baseball and later my own girlfriend, who wasn't Colette, but that's another story. In any case, The Fox and The Cudgel would never fight again, their rivalry forever forestalled by the rapidly shifting fancies which come with adolescence.

THE SUMMER CAME AND WENT; we all started high school. That fall I had a moment of awareness, my first brush with how life's allegiances and foci so easily change: during grades six through eight, our lives had revolved around the collecting and trading of those four-color, newsprint flights of fancy. We scoured yard sales; we begged our parents to take us to the big flea markets on the other side of Columbia. What struck me, however, on the day I sold my collection to Barrett was how I felt no remorse, how objects that'd once held such meaning for me now seemed like ephemera. Even, I realized in a cascading epiphany, the comics I'd helped make.

When I told him I'd gotten rid of my collection, my Dad scolded me. "You can't see it now, Tim," he said, "but one day you'll regret not having kept all them funny books."

For all our nascent artistic endeavors, Barrett would be

the one to pursue a truly creative path—he's now a TV writer and producer in LA, probably makes so much money it's shameful. I still get a thrill whenever I see his name in the credits, which is often. My buddy. He moved away in tenth grade. We haven't spoken in a couple of decades.

MY OWN ADULT life's turned out less creative and lucrative, but hey, advertising's a profitable business, too: I have a house, a family, a white picket fence, if only in metaphor; there's even a couple of awards on the mantlepiece in recognition of my work. More than any one man could need. A writer, like I'd always dreamed, working in creative group environments, as though the comics cabal had been a signpost toward my eventual adult destiny.

And, I still make up stories, but only as a hobby—flash fiction, a novella, a half-baked attempt at a commercial thriller I wrote last year. Maybe I'll send something out. One day. Or not.

As for Gerald, at a certain point he went down a precipitous path, one much darker than our innocent plot-lines of heroes versus villains. The last few times I saw him, as freshmen at Southeastern University—*fifteen years ago, the memoirist thinks with stark horror*—Gerald's principal ambition had become consciousness expansion, a predilection that'd begun in high school when he started running with a rough redneck crowd; rank intoxication more apt a depiction of his activities. He'd take partying, in this case too innocuous a term, to ruinous levels.

Once, toward the end of that first college semester, he showed me a needle mark in the crook of his elbow. Grinning, as though he'd been awarded a depraved merit badge.

I was shocked. "Dude, is that what I think it is?"

"Yeah." By then his eyes had taken on a permanent, glassy sheen, and they rolled back in his head in a sense-memory, I supposed, of doing the drug. "Like nothing I've ever tried, man. Like heaven."

Look: I drank. I smoked some stuff. But this was hardcore. "You're nuts."

Dismissive. "I won't get hooked. I'm different."

He didn't return for sophomore year.

Much later I heard through my mother's gossip grapevine that he'd been imprisoned for distribution of controlled substances, including that which he'd injected "for the experience," as Gerald justified his so-called experimentation. Twenty years, they gave him. Childhood's end; party's over.

"What are you working on these days?" my wife asked me the other night. Despite the solitude that writing demands, she supports my scribbling. "You haven't given me anything to read in a while."

"Just a comic book story," I said.

"A comic book?" She laughed and waved me off. "Oh, please. What are you really doing?"

I didn't explain, only smiled at her.

After I read what I'd written, a vaguely autobiographical short story I called "Comics Cabal," I sighed and set the piece aside. No huge conflicts, nothing about Gerald and his later problems, no drama. No cascading epiphanies.

I decided to look up my old friend. They say write what you know. But what did I know? Nothing. After all, what kind of friend had I been?

I phoned his mother. The news, positive. "Gerald's doing real good, Tim. Got him a job. Keeping up with things."

"Is he—okay?"

She understood what I meant. "He goes to his meetings every day. Says his group helps keep him on an even keel."

Relieved, I said, "Please give him my number, if you would. Been too long."

She sighed. "I know he'd love to hear from you. He was talking about you just the other day."

"He was?"

"Yes—after he found a box of old funny books up in the attic."

I felt the years weighing down upon my soul. "He kept his comics all this time?"

"No," she said. "Not all of them. Only the ones that meant something to him." She paused, cleared her throat. "Look here, don't tell him I told you this, but... when he saw them things, he got real upset. Cried like a baby."

I didn't need to ask which ones she meant. "Did you read them?"

"No—they didn't look like much to me. Didn't even have any color."

I laughed, thanked her, hung up. I didn't call Gerald right away—instead, I went back to my own story. I had our origin down cold; what I'd write now was the moment of redemption—the triumph of a hero, one who'd at last bested the villain within him. Crowd goes wild.

earworm

BAND CAMP WEEK GOT OFF ON A DRAMATIC NOTE when, on that hot late summer morning on the way to Rockland College, Missy LaFreniere's car skipped off the road and cleaved itself unto a telephone pole. Sudden, the crumpled wreck spinning onto the shoulder. A spray of glass into the air that looked like water. The screaming of brakes on asphalt from all the cars following her. My friends and I, all freshman woodwinds being driven in a van by my father, also screamed.

Daddy stomped the brakes and cussed all high-voiced, like he'd had the mess scared out of him. As he wrestled the van over to the side of the road my head felt funny, like I was in a dream or watching a movie.

Worse than the car wreck, though, was that one of the passengers was this new girl who had moved in right at the end of July, Augusta, but everyone called her Gus; 'Gus, Gus, Gus' you'd hear echoing all around. Instantly accepted and popular among upper- and underclassmen alike, t'was she who sat in the seat in Missy's car in which I should have been sitting. That Gus had been asked by Missy, one of the most popular girls in the band, she who had once befriended pitiful freshman me, only to later trade up for Gus, had hurt.

Missy, who suggested I might could ride with her herself, now acted like she didn't even know me. It was like pulling a rug from under my feet. Would rather have had my nose bashed in, like Missy's, standing outside her car and bleeding and crying.

But I know, I know; nobody'd want to be in a car accident. When it was your shot at being accepted by some of the first chair players in the high school marching band—and as a freshman—I bet you'd endure all sorts of perils and pitfalls, though. Tell truth.

Long story short: Gus got to scream along with Missy LaFreniere. Instead of me. What a gyp.

With the entire convoy of cars in the band caravan now pulled over to the shoulder of the two-lane road not far off the interstate up from Edgewater County, Daddy ordered us to stay put, jumped out and went running up to Melissa's car now sitting crooked to the road. Its headlights were busted and broken, and the radiator grill hissed steam like an angry, cross-eyed dragon. Dark fluids had begun leaking and running onto the grassy shoulder.

The rest of us, Darlynn and two other girls, sat still and quiet for all of ten seconds, watching as a bunch of other people, students and grownups alike, went running by us to Melissa's car.

"This ain't fair," I heard myself blurt. Hating my mother, now, for insisting that Daddy be one of the drivers. "I'm getting out."

"Well, I ain't staying in here—for one thing, it's too durn hot," Darlynn said.

In a flurry, seat belts came flying off the other girls and we all tumbled out.

A regular crowd had gathered, all the rest of the band students piling out of all the cars and running over the way we had. By the time I got there, Daddy and the other men had helped the other girls out of the car. Missy's bloody nose had busted wide open when she'd hit the steering wheel, this despite having had her seatbelt on. It looked like one of Missy's teeth was broken, too.

A local man in muddy work pants and a plaid shirt had come off his front porch across the way, saying he had called 9-1-1. "That's how hard she T-boned that pole," he said of Missy' injuries. Fussing with his Southeastern Redtails ball cap, he repeated, "That's just how hard."

Sweating, all of us stood around in our shorts and tank tops and Keds and Nikes. The South Carolina morning sun blazed hot already, with me wishing I had my sunglasses—I took them off earlier so I could read.

We watched as each of Missy's three passengers, Gus included, stood mostly unhurt and receiving hugs of consolation—in fact, a regular line had formed of folks waiting to hug and console them, in particular a number of the upperclass boys from the drum line.

Another reason to be jealous, now. Boys boys boys, handsome brass players and drummers and oh-my, that feeling I get in my tummy when one of them looks my way.

Gus seemed to be the most poised of the survivors, a cheerful glowing flush to her cheeks, smiling and shrugging and saying repeatedly, "I'm fine—really, I'm fine."

Who glows after a car wreck? No wonder the boys were lined up.

"Missy, what happened?" somebody asked.

Sucking wind as Ms. Tuggle and Mr. Leaphart, our band directors, attended to her bleeding nose, she gurgled that she didn't know. "All I remember is my tires ran off the side, and I jerked the wheel to go back on," sobbing and wailing and gurgling some more. She began saying 'oh my god' and 'I'm so sorry' over and over, and required more comforting and bandages.

It all started to seem too dramatic to me. Attention mongering, how distasteful—instead of being in the marching band, I'm surprised she hadn't chosen being a cheerleader. Missy: full of herself. I was watching them ride along in front of us, could see that they were all laughing and joking and not paying attention.

I'll never be like that when I get to be an upperclassman, so exclusive and snotty and desperately uncool. She's been right nice to me with asking me to ride with her and all, though, and I have to give her that, poor bloody stuck-up Missy, even if she did forget about me.

"That's a good lesson there for when y'all are drivers," Daddy said to me and Darlynn and all the others in earshot. "If you start to go off the road, don't never jerk the wheel like she done. That's what caused her to lose control. Ease your tires back onto the road."

"Yes sir, Mr. Latham," Darlynn said. "We will. Or—we won't, I mean."

"Everybody be thankful it wasn't no worse. Them girls could all be hurt bad now."

Mr. Leaphart sent word we all should go on to the college, that Missy would be taken to the local hospital by an ambulance called by a trooper who had shown up. The excitement waning, band parents and kids all moseyed back to their vehicles.

The ride on over to the college, another ten miles or so down the emerald green tunnels of overhanging trees, so different seeming from all the pine trees back home that I feel like I'm in a different state, almost, goes by quietly, with Daddy humming to himself the way he does when he feels uncomfortable, like when it's a syrupy or sad scene on some TV show, when anybody's crying or upset. He also drove on in through the town real careful, keeping both hands on the wheel and not even waving to people passing him like he would normally back home.

"Missy's embouchure's not gonna be for worth a toot, not with that broke tooth." We were sweating again as we unloaded our luggage and waited to get our room assignments, in dorm rooms where, in the fall, college students would be living; the thought filled me with mysterious anticipation. College seemed a long way off. "No more first chair for her."

"Nope, not worth a durn," my oldest and best-est friend said, going tsk-tsk. "If her teeth ain't right, ain't no way she's gonna make first chair."

"Who, then?"

"Not us." The look on her face said she knew I was right. "Not a freshman."

But a girl could dream.

It all made me want to practice. And see if those upperclassmen would notice an exceptionally strong clarinet player whose teeth weren't busted.

MAYBE THE WORST part about being in the high school marching band—well, aside from a bunch of other problems that may or may not be worth making remarks about, practical matters of fatigue and hardship and heat and boredom—is getting one of the songs we've been rehearsing stuck in my head, which has been happening to both me and Darlynn.

Band camp is a whole 'nother story than car wrecks and

music and earworms: speaking of those cute older boys, during dinner that first night I scheme and plan for love to happen with Forrest Ashby, one of the roadside huggers. A tenor saxophone player (second chair), Forrest is a junior, with brown hair and deep, endless brown-eyed pools of handsome.

Most attractive of all, though, is that he's at ease in his own skin: Forrest glides around, joking and smiling and chatting up everyone, even lowly ninth-grade woodwinds like me. And acting like he's listening to me when I talk, which nobody has ever seemed to do, neither in school nor with my family out in this sticks.

When Forrest smiled at me on the first day of marching band practice and said, 'Hi,' I thought I would collapse into a puddle of girl-muck. "Aren't you as cute as can be."

Feeling like an idiot, I stammered and went 'um' a couple of times, finally saying, "I reckon."

"No reckoning about it," he said with a wink, moving back to his own kind among the other juniors and seniors. He's the student body vice president. Maybe he wants to grow up and be a politician for real.

I know—maybe I'll ask *him* to finally go on a date... if Daddy will let me, that is.

In any case: cleanup of girl-muck on aisle eight, please.

Feeling naughty, after we got our trays of cafeteria food I stealthily watched as he laughed and joked with his other handsome friends, eating their burgers and whooping it up like a group of kids on vacation rather than being here to work, which Mr. Leaphart reminds us about in little speeches he keeps making.

Forrest, you will notice me. You will be mine. And you won't mind, not a bit. You'll see.

Rockland College, where the Byrnes High School marching band goes for its camp, is a small school in the upstate with a campus full of tall shady trees, and it's not as hot as back home in Edgewater County, but still steamy. Being away from home like this feels so different from the usual long, boring summer. Like I'm changing inside, or so I keep telling myself:

I'm not a little girl any more. I'm in high school.

After breakfast on our first full day, but before beginning the morning marching drill, we mill around on the sidewalk outside the dining hall; I'm whispering to Darlynn and Tina Montreat about how I'm going to talk to Forrest today, going to let him know somehow about the way I feel.

They're intrigued but skeptical. "This I got to see," Tina the sourpuss says. "He's already dating somebody."

"Who?"

She shrugs. "I mean, probably dating somebody."

"Oh, hush."

Margaret Tuggle's sister Karen, our new assistant band director, emerges from the dining hall with Mr. Leaphart, who gestured toward the field and gave instructions. Ms. Tuggle, not much older than the senior girls, is a beauty—tall, with a mane of hair pulled back by a paisley bandana that I went over and told her I admired. Ms. Tuggle, as we're supposed to call her, is so pretty she should be in a Virginia Slims ad in *Cosmo*.

She describes the bandana as her lucky one, one she's worn through any number of difficulties. "It's gotten me through tough exams and bad camping trips and bad boyfriends," she says, lowering her voice and laughing all low and knowing; she's a grownup, has 'been around.' "A couple of them, in fact."

"How'd you know they were bad?"

Her face turns sour. "Oh, honey, you find out real quick. If you're lucky, anyway. A couple I didn't find out soon enough..."

"Can I talk to you? About... boyfriends?"

Intrigued, she checks her watch and says, "Sure."

Under a tree by the soccer field, which is still semi-shady and dewy rather than steaming hot as it'd be later, we lean against a picnic table. Ms. Tuggle gestures and orders three of the color guard seniors to go use their fake rifles to mark certain points where our rows are to form on the unlined, grassy field.

"What's going on?"

The words feel sticky in my throat, like they aren't sure they should be sneaking out: I tell her about the second chair saxophone player Forrest Ashby. How I hope romance with him will happen soon—here at band camp—but I don't know how.

"What's the rush, sweetheart?"

"Because," I hear myself blurt, "I think I love him." I felt ashamed by my honesty.

"Oh... Lucy," as though she had to think hard on my name. "It's just a crush. Not love. Not at your age."

"It's like it hurts inside."

"Angel, it'll be fine," she says, putting her hands on my shoulders. "You're as tall as me now—when did that happen?"

I mumble that I don't know.

She sighs and says, look; the best thing I can do is to be myself, to smile and to feel happy inside and out, and that, if Forrest is the right one in the right moment in the right space, maybe it will happen—that the universe will make certain of this outcome.

"The universe?"

"It just means be yourself and think good thoughts, and good things will come to you all on their own, without trying. Do without doing, so to speak. I had a roommate who was into Eastern stuff. Chanting '*aum*' and all that mess. Among other things," she says like a conspirator, miming as though smoking a very small cigarette, none of which I quite understand. "Anyway, it's always better to go with the ones who have the sense and taste to have noticed *you* first, rather than the other way around. Get it?"

"That's what I'm trying to say. *He already did.*"

"Still. My advice holds: let it unfold. Don't force it. 'Aum,'" she says, crossing her eyes and holding her hands together in front of her. "Right?"

"I reckon."

Upon checking her watch again and seeing the rest of the band coming down the sidewalk toward the lush green field, she tousles my hair, making me feel about six years old. "Keep me posted, Lacey," she says, mixing me up with one of the other freshman girls, a flutist. "Remember, don't rush—good things to those who wait."

CATASTROPHE: by late Tuesday, Forrest has hooked up with Augusta, holding hands, walking to lunch and to dinner with their arms around one another.

No. Anyone but Gus!

I cry all night and feel stomach-sick Wednesday morning, which gets me out of marching practice.

Ms. Tuggle asks if I'd had 'that fish' last night in the

dining hall. I had, and she says it made her a little queasy as well. "Any news on the romantic front?"

"No," almost breaking down. "He's with Gus, now," sounding pitiful.

"Well. Lots of cute boys out there." Her tone turning stern, like that of a teacher, she tells me to get myself on the mend by the afternoon. That Mr. Leaphart needs us all at our best, if we're to field a championship band.

By lunch I'm fine. I go and eat with everyone like nothing's happened. In afternoon rehearsal, I refuse to think about the fact that Forrest sits *so close* behind me, honking away on his tenor sax, yet cannot see me. Right here. Cannot see the *me* who loves him. Band camp sucks.

THERE'S a traditional party and dance on Friday night, before we're to head back home to boring old Edgewater County. I stand against the wall with Darlynn and Tina and Lacey to watch as the upperclassmen all boogie to disco tunes and slow ones, too.

Handsome Barrett O'Steen, mellophone, broad-shouldered dark-haired, sidles up next to me. Holds out his hand.

"C'mon, lonesome dove—let's cut a rug. What say you?"

My heart starts beating. Hard. I haven't paid him much attention, but: He smells like aftershave. A junior. Like Forrest.

Oh, my god!

His hand, warm and dry, takes mine and he leads me onto the cleared floor of the rehearsal hall, our instruments and chairs and music stands all pushed into a big cluster along the back wall. Mr. Leaphart sits there with a record player acting as DJ. We shimmy and shake to KC and the

Sunshine band, an old song, until next, a slow one—The Commodores.

Gulp.

"We're already here, after all." His voice comes as a purr. "We may not pass this way again, my little love."

Our chins rested on one another's shoulders, he holds me close, our bodies touching, warm and damp.

In an instant Forrest is a memory. Barrett's on my mind now, his smell and warmth from our dance still on me the rest of the night and the whole drive home that next day; I didn't want to shower.

In the parking lot as we unload and my parents wave to me, I catch his eye, and he mine. "I'll call you," he mouths across the asphalt.

My knees go weak—it's for real.

As the weeks progress, our halftime show starts to come together; we march every day until school starts, then three practices a week after class in the afternoon.

We perform at the football games, of course, but the reason the band marches isn't for the football team: it's to do well in different competitions leading up to the State Contest, which is what Mr. Leaphart calls The Big Show. Our songs are 'Fanfare for the Common Man' and '25 or 6 to 4,' and then our showstopper, 'Live and Let Die,' which Mr. Leaphart chose because he says it represents two of the most important cultural touchstones of the 60s, The Beatles and James Bond, all mashed up together.

Barrett has been calling every night. Our first date will be the first football game, in a sense: he's asked me to sit with him on the bus ride to the game and back.

"You look gorgeous tonight," Barrett says as we trundle along highway 79 toward Andrew Jackson High, all bundled up in our woolen uniforms and sweating in the Indian summer warmth. "Truly."

Every time he opens his mouth he gives me butterflies, but especially with a compliment like that. "I do?"

"A queen—my little freshman queen." And a quick secret smooch.

Dizzy.

He takes my hand. I lean my head on his shoulder. He sighs.

THE FOOTBALL GAME is now half over, and the home crowd at Andrew Jackson High seems to like our halftime show, especially 'Live and Let Die,' which gets people whooping and hollering.

A certain kind of feeling at the football games, the light from those white stadium lights and the colorful band of sky and the deepening blue indigo of the coming night, and later in the season the nip in the air, the sound of the crowd and the people with their paper cups of popcorn and soda, all of which feels different now that I'm part of the show instead of a mere spectator sitting with Daddy and Timmy. The high school football game. Friday night. In a little town like ours, people treat it like church.

Loading into the buses, however, there come words with the other band, who had beaten us last year in the State Contest. A fight nearly breaks out between the two drum lines, both sides teeming with cocky upperclassmen but especially the timpani players, but the fight's diffused by Mr. Leaphart and one of the football coaches, both of whom hollering *Stop Stop Break it Up* like angry grownups, which seems out of character for Mr. Leaphart, and scarier than the fight itself.

THE BUSES BUMP along through the Pisgette National Forrest which covers the western half of the county; forty miles on the two-lane road takes us an hour. Bo-ring—unless you're sitting with your handsome boyfriend.

After a few minutes the boisterous bus of teenagers settles into more of a quiet, murmuring state of being, including Barrett, who in the darkness begins kissing me and putting his tongue all in my mouth, which I try to reciprocate, but he's kissing me for so long—*is this right? is this how it's done? I will have to ask Ms. Tuggle*—that the spit keeps sliding down my throat and making me choke because I can't swallow it quick enough.

Finally he retracts his tongue. "Mm-mm, Lucy-loo," he whispers, hot against my neck. "You taste so good."

I try to answer but all I can do is gurgle. I need a spit-valve, like on one of the brass instruments. "This is—um. Yummy."

He puts his arm all the way around and up under my boobs, which makes me draw in my breath, sharp. Goes 'mm-mm' again. Smooches me some more.

He whispers, sudden and urgent and super quiet: "Hey—you wanna play?"

I'm not sure what he means—our instruments? "Huh?"

"Like this." Barrett throws his vinyl band windbreaker across our laps. He twists his neck all around, but nobody cares: we are unnoticed, because with two other couples in the seats around us, all I can hear is soft smacking, slurping and rustling.

He fumbles around under the windbreaker. "What say you, my little queen?"

More wet deep smooching, until he takes both my hands in his—a sweet gesture.

Moves them. Onto his lap. Onto a spongy rigidity there, jutting up hot and soft-sticky. It's his—his—*thing*. "*Oh*," I cry out, yanking back my hands.

"Hey, cool it, cool it."

Ms. Tuggle, sitting up in the front seat with her arms folded, twists around. "What the heck's going on back there?"

"Forrest farted a green one," Jeff Barfield yells. "We need oxygen!"

An explosion of laughter and catcalls; everyone starts throwing their gloves and hats at Forrest, a blizzard of objects.

The driver flips on the interior lights. Ms. Tuggle calls out for everyone to *Hush, hush*; for everyone to *settle down*.

In the ruckus I slide across the bench seat to the window, away from Barrett. I push his windbreaker off my lap.

The lights go back off. "Are we on? Or what?"

"No. That's—gross."

"Gross?" he whispers. "Damn."

I like him and think the kissing is wonderful and new and that makes me so gooey inside, but his thing? Already? Too soon. Too—weird. "I'm—not ready for that."

He fumbles around noisily under the windbreaker, throwing it off and sitting here stony and quiet but for one bitter and hateful word: "Weirdo."

That's the last of my dating Barrett—I won't have my first time 'playing' on a ratty old school bus, with people farting and laughing and all doing the same thing. You talk about weird.

Besides, at these contests coming up, Mr. Leaphart needs us at our 'unmitigated' best, as he keeps saying, and so I don't care if Barrett or any other boy—well, maybe Forrest—asks me to sit with him on the bus: I will have to think long and hard about it before saying yes. Not unless it's to hold hands and kiss and have a romance, and we are up front about all that from the git-go.

A real date. A real boyfriend. Not a bad one. That's what I want. Maybe I need my version of Ms. Tuggle's doo-rag. Yes. Before the State Contest next weekend, I'll get Daddy to take me to the mall and instead of a record like usual, I'll get a paisley bandana from the Levi's store on the second level.

Ms. Tuggle's advice—about not-doing, and letting the universe guide things instead of trying to force the matter—has gotten stuck in my head. At least that's better than a song like 'Live and Let Die,' which I used to like. By the time the season is over, I won't care if I ever hear that one again.

eye of the vandal

WE SCURRY ALONG THE CURBSIDE OF THE SCHOOL parking lot like skittering crabs. Skirting glowing pools of ocher light from the tall street lamps, we seem like we're up to something. Like men on a dangerous mission.

Not really. It's nighttime—late—but if anyone sees us, it doesn't matter. We're not up to anything. It's only pretend danger. Like playing army.

But I haven't done that in ages; we're fourteen, now. About to go to high school.

Actually, I don't know what we're doing. What my friend Troy has in mind. But I'm about to find out.

When I stray too far into the light, he yanks me deeper into the gloom of the long breezeway beside which students get onto the yellow school buses.

"We mustn't be seen."

"No, commander—forgive me."

We're both doing British accents. Earlier with his dad we watched a movie called *The Wild Geese,* with the Richards—Burton and Harris—plus the guy who plays James

Bond. All seasoned mercenaries, sent on a suicide mission. Definitely not playtime. "*I mustn't be captured.*"

"If we're found out, we'll be forced to shoot each other," I whispered.

"We'll have no choice."

We shake on it.

In the breezeway, Troy, who's been coy about the backpack, squats and fusses inside it. Sees me watching him.

Back in my normal voice. "What's in the bag?"

Still with the accent. "You'll find out, yank."

We crouch in the inky shadows at the rear entrance of the school, facing away from the highway and the front lobby. Inside I can see long rows of bright yellow underclassmen lockers, which come August we'll use for our books and such.

A young summer, but already muggy. That's South Carolina—you live here and it's hot and humid; you go to movies or sit inside to read or watch TV. Neither band nor football camp has started. Neither Independence Day nor my family's annual beach trip has happened yet. We're still getting used to being out of school.

Restless, at times. Like tonight.

"You know how I said I wanted to spray-paint some truth onto these walls?" He rummages; metal on metal, clanking. "Some remarks about that Natasha chick?"

Earlier in the week we walked over here to watch marching band rehearsals in the empty asphalt parking lot, itself as big as the stadium football field. When the band took a break Troy tried flirting with some of the older girls, but got snubbed by a blonde in the color guard. Embarrassed, he said he'd get her back. Would teach her a lesson.

"Dang—you're really gonna do it?"

"Why not?"

Troy wants to vandalize the school—our new school.

Before we've attended a single class. My stomach drops into my tennis shoes. "That's pretty harsh."

Standing in the hot summer night air at the high school, Troy falls quiet. He's staring at the spray paint can. Shakes his head. Says he's changed his mind about telling the world that Natasha's a stuck-up bitch. "More I think about it, might be obvious who did it."

"It's not like they knew you."

"Bunch of her friends saw me chatting her up."

I nod, remembering how the gaggle of girls laughed at him.

"But I got something else in mind."

From the knapsack Troy pulls out his sleek, blue-black Crosman 357-4 CO_2 powered air pistol. All I've ever owned is a secondhand, pump-action BB rifle that holds plenty of shot, but often jams. Troy's Crosman looks like the gun they put into the hands of bad-ass movie cops like Dirty Harry, with a thick wooden handle and a long barrel. Troy has let me shoot it at squirrels and birds and bottles, which it shatters with ease.

I ask him what's to be done with the weapon. "It's too dark for target practice."

"Move away from these windows, and get ready to find out."

OVER THE LAST year I've become a regular fixture at Troy's house, a split level contemporary with a pool; a place at the Monckton table in the dining room is often mine.

His family lives in the newer subdivision near the school, houses built in what had been nothing but woods now sheared away, the stumps ground down and the trees forgotten. His folks are so sweet and kind you would think they're Southerners like the rest of us, but they're not—they're from up north, in Pennsylvania. City folk. His dad works at the nuclear plant over by the river. He's smart. None of them sound like they're from South Carolina. It's cool and different to hang out around them.

Troy's room sits on one side of their house, far away from the master bedroom where his parents sleep. It gives him privacy that I've envied ever since we became friends, last year in seventh grade. He even has his own door to come and go. Before creeping out of Troy's room we waited until the coast was clear, and only after he making sure his parents had zonked out.

About eleven, his dad, sleepy and with a book under his arm, checked on us. We were playing records and looking at a set of sexy playing cards Troy kept secreted under his mattress. When the door opened he tossed an album cover, *KISS Alive*, onto the cards. Casual. A smooth operator.

"Hey, Pop—you gonna crash?"

His dad nodded. "Now, don't rattle our windowsills with those rock records."

"You love it, Pop."

"I rue the day we bought you that stereo set." Grumbling, a routine, an act between them I had seen a few times already. Unlike mine, his dad had gone to college. Spoke like some TV dad, a flat accent, almost a different language. "And I don't recommend staying up all night. Sleep is important to your health. To everyone's—get my drift?"

"Sure, Pops."

He shut the door.

"When their bedside radio goes off, it means they're gone."

"How will we hear it?"

"I'll go and check. But not yet."

Instead of music, his parents listen to people talking on the radio. Watch TV shows on PBS like *William F. Buckley's Firing Line.* "So your folks go off the same time as the radio does?"

Troy squinted with what my country grandmother would call devil eyes. "You making fun of my family?"

Cold inside. "Naw, man."

"Better not."

"I didn't mean nothing." Compared to Troy, I sound all country. "Anything."

He chucked me in the bicep with a hard knuckle. "Keep it that way."

"Ow."

Troy said how his mom takes over-the-counter sleep aids, a common brand with ads on TV and in magazines. "But sometimes my dad gets up to drink a glass of milk."

Another half hour went by. Troy crept out in his sock feet.

He returned from the re-con patrol. "Now we can prowl."

Troy grabbed a small knapsack, olive green, like they sell at the Army-Navy store in downtown Columbia. He eased open the outside door, careful not to rattle the heavy wooden blinds over the window.

"What we gonna do?"

He snickered. "Get into some crap."

Out on the sidewalk. Nighttime. Crickets. A dog barking somewhere way off. Everybody asleep. No cars. The glow from the high school parking lot a half mile away, eerie and unnatural above the trees. A row of mature red tips separated the yard from the house next door. Quiet as mice, we stole along the flagstone pathway leading around front.

Staying over at Troy's is also cool because of being closer to the new interstate junction, only a couple of miles away, either by bicycle or Troy's rad navy blue Yamaha moped. A Hardee's and two gas stations have been built there, with ground broken for what's gonna be a Holiday Inn and another restaurant. My dad says it's gonna be a McDonald's.

One of the filling stations, a Gulf, captured our imagination—Mr. Monckton had stopped there for gas, and in the men's room Troy discovered a "kick ass" condom machine.

"With French ticklers, too."

I knew about rubbers, but not French ticklers. I didn't let Troy know I had no clue how to use one. "How much are they?"

"Fifty cents apiece." He pulled a couple of quarters out of his cutoff shorts and jangled them in my face. "When school starts, we're gonna need a good stash of those."

"You—really think so?"

He looked at me like, duh. "Timmy, haven't you seen these high school chicks?" This was before Natasha had shot him down. "They put out, brother."

Troy claimed to have gotten pretty far with a couple of girls in our own grade, the two prettiest ones besides the girl I liked. He said one had kissed him with tongues, but also more: Mandy Portee had let him put his hand down into her shorts. He said it had been hot and damp down there. That her musky fragrance lingered on his fingertips.

I seesawed between feeling titillation and revulsion. "Why?"

"I didn't want to wash it off. Her smell did something to me."

"Was it—cool?"

"What, you mean you don't know?"

I stammered, of course I did. "I just meant hers. Was *hers* cool."

His eyes seemed to know I was lying. "Of course it was."

Besides getting to kiss Colette Carrolton at that one party, I still haven't found a real girlfriend. For one thing, I haven't gotten over Colette, but she's going with Greg Rinker, and so that's that. And if it wasn't happening with her I didn't want anyone, like the song on the *Saturday Night Fever* soundtrack, the one with the French horns.

But last weekend Troy insisted we go get the condoms, me riding on the back of his moped. The macadam of the county road rattled my braces. I hoped my dad wouldn't be getting gas or a fast food sandwich. He would wonder what we were doing all the way over there.

But before we got even halfway to the Gulf the skies turned smudgy gray, even darker in the direction of the freeway interchange. We stopped and debated the merits of the mission, one I wasn't sure I wanted to achieve anyway. I'm still not sure what a rubber does, exactly.

"Looks like we're gonna get wet."

"Yeah... not worth getting soaked." A far-off peal of thunder made it seem as though nature concurred. "We'll get them next week."

I shrugged. "We got all summer."

Troy, nodding. "Damn straight. School doesn't start in like, forever."

Onto a smoother road, paved for a subdivision under construction, the ride became more comfortable. Being late in the day, the workers had all finished and gone home. The naked framing of the houses, standing forlorn under the gloomy sky, seemed spooky.

A model home had been all-but finished. It sat right behind a big brick sign, PECAN RIDGE ESTATES. Troy turned into the subdivision.

"Where you going?"

"To see if it's unlocked."

Troy drove into the yard where the driveway would be poured, and we almost fell off in the loose dirt. We got off and he pushed the moped around back.

The doors, locked. He cussed.

"We don't want to get caught anyway," I said.

"Yeah, but we need to do something."

In the backyard, well hidden from the main road, Troy picked up a rock. "Check this out." He reared back and flung it toward a window.

At the shatter of glass, my heart jumped into my throat. "Damn, dude."

Troy's face turned bright red. He laughed through his teeth. "That was awesome."

He grabbed up a chunk of red brick from the sandy yard where grass would one day grow. Chucked it dead center through the middle of another window. Laughed.

A car, approaching on the highway. I held my breath. It kept going.

"C'mon, dude. That's enough."

Looking around like he wanted to break one more, he said, "Yeah. I guess."

Back on the moped, skinny pine trees streaked by on both sides. Trash had collected in the high weeds where the county needed to mow.

At supper his mom asked what we had been doing.

"Playing baseball."

"Baseball? With whom?"

Glancing at me, Troy started making up this whole story

about a sandlot ball game, one that never occurred. Named other kids I'd never met, that far as I know didn't live in the neighborhood at all.

"We woulda won, too," he concluded. "But the others, they got scared of a rain cloud that came up."

"Since when are little boys scared of rain?"

"They were chicken."

"That's too bad." She smiled at me, making my face flush hot. "Maybe you can play again tomorrow."

Troy's got some imagination. I think he when he grows up he should write TV shows, like my friend Barrett says he wants to do. I never know what to expect out of Troy, like wanting to sneak out of his house late at night on a mission most mysterious.

STANDING a few yards back from the double door school entrance I feel exposed, but nobody can see back in this shadowy corner of the bus parking lot. Not this late at night. The world is asleep. A nasty smell, high and sickly sweet, from the nearby dumpster tickles my nose.

"Watch what this thing can do." Troy aims and fires the gun at the narrow window to the right of the doorway, a whole volley of shots. The Crosman is a repeater pistol; the gas propels the BBs at a high rate of speed.

I wince, expecting to hear glass breaking. But the window, it doesn't shatter.

"Damn it." Troy cusses some more. "What the hell."

We approach the doors. Troy's weapon has indeed shattered the window, but it's hanging there still in one piece. Starry patterns radiate out from tiny BB holes. A crackling sound comes off it.

"Sounds like Rice Krispies."

"A work of art." But Troy sighed. "The glass, it must be coated in plastic. Or some crap."

I don't like all this vandalism. People like Troy, who break stuff without worrying about who's to clean it up, I don't know: it just seems wrong. "Guess we ought to get out of here."

"Nope. Now it's your turn."

"My turn?"

"Take out the other side, soldier."

I can't say no—I'll seem uncool, even chicken. "Maybe we should get out of here."

It's got to match, as he explains. But more important: "Don't wimp out."

Ouch. "But I don't wanna. That made a lotta noise."

"Wimp."

"But dude—c'mon."

He insists, brandishing the butt of the gun at me. "Here."

We retake our positions of safety. Holding the gun straight out in front of me, I squint. Aim. My hand, it's shaking.

I squeeze off a single shot.

In a flash the BB ricochets back toward me, a golden streak in the night—and strikes my face.

My eye.

I cry out, dropping the gun onto the asphalt.

"*Be quiet.*" Troy snatches up the Crosman. "You better not have broken it."

I probe and find the eyeball, still intact—I can see. But a welt, rising up just below on my cheekbone. "That hurt like hell."

Dusting grit from the pistol. "It bounced the freak back on you. Pretty wild."

My heart pounds. How close did I come to losing an eye?

Not to mention how we'd get busted, too, if I had to go to the hospital. Explain myself to his parents, the doctor, and others—like my own folks.

At the thought of telling my dad what we're out here doing, I grow cold inside.

"What went wrong, you big moron?"

"I shot at it like you told me to."

Examining the windows, we still hear the crackling in Troy's. Mine? Still intact.

Troy bangs the target with the barrel of the gun. "Holy crap."

"*What?*"

"It's Plexiglas. Explains why the BB bounced off."

My eye socket throbs. "They must've already replaced this one."

"What a gyp." Troy, disappointed. "What a bunch of crap."

I feel angry. And scared, now. We're vandalizing the high school, and we haven't even started here yet. Colette Carrolton's gonna see this damage when she comes to band practice. How stupid of us.

Of me.

"Let's get outta here. I need to put some ice on this."

"Yeah. Sorry, bro."

"It doesn't hurt that much," a lie.

"I meant about your window not breaking. That's a raw deal."

I feign disappointment. It's not every day you almost shoot out your own eye. "It wasn't meant to be, I guess."

On the walk back to his house, I decide the next time Troy wants to break somebody's windows, I'll tell him no; I'll remind him about my eye. My grandfather once told me how one of the worst sins is to do wrong after you already know what you're doing is wrong—because if *you* know, then God knows.

I consider telling all this to Troy, but he'll just say it's crap. His folks don't go to church.

Besides, I need him to make up a good story about what happened to my face, which come tomorrow will sport a shiner. Another baseball game, maybe.

It occurs to me: I'll tell my folks we got into a fight with some other kids. Or, maybe, I'll tell everyone Troy and I got into the fight—maybe over a girl. But how we're still friends. And that it's all cool.

Coming back around the corner to his house, with a shock I realize we'll need to come up with a story sooner rather than later: the light is on in the living room. A silhouetted figure, hands on hips, peers into the nighttime—Mr. Monckton.

"He checked on us." Troy shifts the knapsack from one shoulder to the other. "My dad and that milk of his."

I'm not worried. I'm sure my friend will know what to say. He always does. And, if not, I guess it'll be up to me to concoct a story.

I know: we'll tell his dad it was so hot we couldn't sleep; we got bored. That we were playing a game, one we made up using a BB gun and a can of spray paint stolen out of the garage. A game boys like us play together, deep in the suburban nighttime, when everyone else—even God, I hoped—is fast asleep.

i puked at karoake

I AM AT THE POINT OF NO RETURN, BUT THE DOOR to the sidewalk will not yield. I push my whole body against the reinforced glass, the cold, aluminum handle, the sturdy frame. Solid. Impenetrable.

My stomach convulses.

Sissy—Lucy—hold it together.

"*Pull*," the doorman says, gravelly and bored. Exasperated, he's enervated by the routine. "Jesus, lady, it says it right there above the handle." He tucks his cigarette into the corner of his mouth and *pulls* the door open for me.

Outside. Cold air on my burning cheeks. I stagger over to a lamppost covered with tattered flyers for bands and bars and more good times to be had. I lean against the pole, trying to catch my breath. It's no good at first, then the cold air seems to cleanse me.

Maybe I'll be okay after all. But then I think about the taste of that last shot, which is still at the back of my teeth.

"Oh-my-god," a female voice says as I spew all over the sidewalk, a plume that is foamy, dark, bitter. I eruct with window-rattling force, the gaseous excretion replaced by another liquid torrent. The couple walking by, neatly dressed middle-agers—the guy looks a little like my dad—sport expressions which betray their revulsion. They hotfoot it on down the block, snickering.

"*Oof*," I say to their retreating backs. "*Gah.*"

Traffic rolling past, yellow light from the blinking stickman on the crosswalk warning, amber neon from the beer signs in the windows of the other bars and restaurants here in the college ghetto. Exhaust, black and greasy, from a bus lumbering along. A prowler rolling past, the young uniformed guys inside eyeballing me with their cop eyes.

The doorman peeks out. "You need me to call a cab, GF?" He is nicer, now—an older guy, thick-limbed, a man hired to handle situations with poise, to keep matters from getting out of hand.

"A cab? Nuh-uh."

"Yeah? No? You look like you're about ready to punch out for the night."

I wipe my mouth on the sleeve of my deep purple, form-fitting T-shirt. I bought it today for karaoke night, for my big moment. The shirt has glitter imbedded in the fabric. I've been sparkling under the UV lights in the ceiling of the bar, which during the rest of the week is an ordinary Irish pub. Not on Wednesdays, though. On this night a transformation occurs. "I'm not leaving. I haven't *sung* yet, motherfucker."

He's unfazed by my profane demeanor. "And you *won't* sing, either. Not if Mistress Beatrix thinks you're gonna hurl all over her microphone."

"What she don't know won't hurt her." My throat is stinging with bile. I'm fumbling in my purse for a breath mint. "I'm fine, now."

"You think she doesn't know? About you?"

"How could she?"

"Mistress Beatrix knows all."

I cut my eyes sidelong at the doorman. The karaoke stage is all the way at the back of the long, narrow bar, which is packed: Wednesdays with Mistress Beatrix, the best karaoke in town. Legendary, even. Some weeks they have to turn people away at the door. Mistress Beatrix, she's working, doing her business. She doesn't know from squat about what's going on out here.

"If you're so potted that you puked already, then she knows."

"Bullcrap."

"Weren't you up there singing along with everybody? Right up front? Top of your lungs?"

I nod.

"Going *woo-hoo*?"

"Uh-huh."

"Dancing around?" He does a light-footed pirouette, graceful and delicate for a man of his bulk.

Grim: "*Yes.*"

"Kiss anyone on the mouth? Anyone you don't know?"

"No!" The only person I've kissed tonight is my friend Esther, earlier when we were slinky-dancing to 'Purple Rain'—and maybe my other friend LaKeesha, too, come to think of it: I sort-of remember everyone cheering for us, catcalling and whoop-whooping in the middle of someone else's song. LaKeesha is one hot box of chocolates. She's everybody's favorite, sexy, getting up there and grinding herself out some Macy Gray.

"Lose any clothes yet?"

I look down: My sweater, once tied around my hips, is missing! "*No,*" a lie.

The doorman looks sour. "That's three out of five," he says. "At *least.*" His disapproval is palpable. "Even without the shouting-at-your-shoes routine you just pulled, little sister."

Who does this fool think he is? Three out of five what? "Don't you worry about it. This is my big night," through a stinging, acid belch. "Just lemme back in."

"Big night? You're here almost every week."

"Yeah." Staring him down with my big eyes, the ones people say are my best attribute. "But not up there."

Inside someone is warbling along to 'Rhiannon.' Earlier, this dreadlocked hippy cat did a droning Radiohead dirge that went on so long it nearly started a drink-throwing riot. People don't come here to karaoke night for that artsy-fartsy crap—they come for the singalongs and feelgoods everybody knows.

I look at Mistress Beatrix, in her six-inch death-stilettos and the tailored, sharp business suit that makes her look as crisp as a fresh C-note from the loading dock of the Philadelphia mint. She clutches an ever-present riding crop in her gloved left hand, occasionally tapping it against her thigh in time to the beat—if, that is, she's enjoying the particular tune that someone's chosen for their big moment.

The doorman, muscled and tatted, with muttonchops and a red hair afro, is smiling at me, cruel, a twinkle in his eyes. "You're a virgin," meaning, I understand, in the karaoke sense.

"Uh-huh." No shit, Sherlock—that's why I was really knocking them back earlier, letting the guys buy me the shots and the beers. Nerves, I said to myself. But this dude doesn't need to know all that. "I made a point of letting *her* know, too," pointing at Mistress Beatrix, a small tremor visible in the tip of my finger.

"I *see*."

I struggle to unwrap an ancient, watermelon Jolly Rancher I've found in the bottom of my bag. I start for the door with a stagger-step, nearly coming out of my wedges. I decide to kick them off, leaving the shoes on the sidewalk. The frayed seams of my Diesels are dragging, toes peeking out like pink little sausages with the tips painted teal.

"Look here," he says, holding the door open for me. "I can get you a cab in, like, five minutes."

'Little Miss Can't Be Wrong' rendered in a *basso profundo* timbre hits me in the face. Mistress Beatrix is standing at parade rest off to the side, lit eerily from below by her luminescent laptop screen. The stage lights are spinning green-blue-purple-red. My head is spinning right along with the colors. "Do what?"

"They even take credit cards," the doorman adds.

"Who?"

"The cabs."

I smirk at him. "I don't need no cab. You just get ready to represent, buster. Peace out." I have sibilance issues. It sounds like *buzzzter* and *peezzzout*.

"Okay, then."

I stumble through the drinkers and the dancers, the anticipatory mass of stagestruck amateurs: the three-minute pop stars, the happy-drunk ladies and the good-time Charlies who eye them with lusty appreciation. The biker/cowboy with the eye makeup who does Hank, both Senior and Junior; the skinny, introverted bookworm by day who kicks up his heels and *becomes* Michael Stipe ripping through "What's the Frequency, Kenneth" or "Radio Free Europe"; the two lanky, bespectacled Indian hep-cats—twins—who always do show-stopping, choreographed showtune duets; the heavyset chick with the fishnets and aqua hair who does Souxsie and The Cure and Morrissey. They are like family to me already. They are the stars, the regulars—Mistress Beatrix and her little teacher's-pets.

And then there's me, captain of the the B-team. The self-help patient looking to conquer some ineffable anxiety, waiting for the chance to stand up in front of them all. To show them my personality, my own stage persona, perfected in the mirror, long practice sessions that started back when I was a little girl.

Oh shit: I can't remember what song I put on my slip. I mean, it's one of three I was mulling over—damn if I can remember which one, though.

Somebody steps on my little toe. I barely notice it.

I feel strong: I'll be ready no matter which tune I chose. I am sparkling, again. I can feel that Mistress Beatrix is about to call my name.

I order one more Michelob Ultra to wet my whistle. The lager is cold as it hits my stomach, which feels good now that it's empty.

I glance back to see the doorman flash a laser pointer three times at me; I smile and wave at him.

Then I turn back to see Mistress Beatrix looking in my direction, her lips pursed. Her blueblack hair and pale makeup give her the appearance of a ghostly headmistress—a severe one. She fixes me with a stare. Her demeanor is officious, brusque. My heart leaps into my throat as she picks up a song-slip. Taps the riding crop against her chin as she scrutinizes it. Looks at her computer screen, then squints at the slip again. The wannabe Spin Doctor, an extremely large African-American man in his forties, jumps around in gratitude for the heartfelt cheers and the applause.

Mistress Beatrix appears to sigh; she tosses the slip into the also-ran pile at her feet. She selects another, which turns out to be that of my friend Esther, who's chosen a Dixie Chicks anthem. Everybody claps for her as she bounces up on the stage in her tube top and cute little cowboy hat. She put in her slip after I did, though, that little twerp. How come she gets picked before me?

I lean against the bar for the rest of the night, waiting to get called up, but it never happens. Then it's three o'clock, the harsh fluorescent house lights wash out my already pale countenance, making everyone look like an extra in a George Romero zombie flick. A pall of gray smoke hangs over everything as those of us left shuffle out into the chill. The crashing of glass as the barbacks empty the trash cans. Laughter and conversation, hugs, smiles, "See y'all next week," all that closing time crap.

"How'd it go?" The doorman is sitting at the corner of the bar, drinking a Diet Pepsi and flipping through yesterday's sports section. "Your big moment."

"Fuck you," I say.

"Hey," frowning at me. "Uncool, little sister."

"Whatever."

"See you next week?"

I shrug and go looking for my shoes. Now my little toes are black with grime from the bar floor. Yuck.

I think back on it the next day, about my skipped song slip. All I can figure is that it must have been an oversight, a mix-up, a flaw, a crack in the shell of Mistress Beatrix's studied, professional karaoke façade. She would surely be mortified to know that I noticed her blunder. Maybe next Wednesday I'll point out this oversight to her. Or, maybe not. After all, I don't want to make a bad impression. I'm trying to sing a song, here.

the blogosphere version

We've lost touch, but only in the tactile sense.

Oh, sure, we keep up. But with each passing season, the gulf widens since the days of the meaningful meatspace relationship I shared with my college roommate and confidant and competitor; the tug of the Tugg.

Nostalgia. At least not errant nostalgia. We were good buds on every level. Still are.

Read an article which theorized about those relationships, adolescence to early adulthood friendships, being the ones that stick with us, often when the people themselves don't. Life gets in the way. But like I said—we keep up.

In my case, Jerome Tuggle, a Columbia cousin to the family I knew from Edgewater County, was more than a friend who provided context about the burgeoning mystery that was impending adulthood. His late-night, smoke-fueled rants and digressions inspired me in such myriad ways I'd be embarrassed to recount them all here. His analytical mind got my own gears grinding in a meaningful way. Where I had come from out in the sticks as the son of working class folks,

Tugg's father had been a Southeastern University professor of some renown who had inculcated scholarship in his children from an early age. I learned as much from my college roommate as I did many of my teachers.

Tugg has gone on to become a hotshot lawyer, although for a time in undergrad he made noise, a fair amount, about really and truly, deep-down, wanting to write. His father had been a modern and contemporary literary scholar who taught and wrote and brought famous writers to town. Tugg told me a story about wandering into his living room as a little kid to find a man with wild hair and mustache sitting on the couch, talking with his father and smoking up a storm. "God, I love to smoke," he recalled Kurt Vonnegut saying. And there'd been others like that. Writing ought to have been in my friend's blood.

IMAGINE, then, my pleasure and surprise one morning, the *ding* pulling me out of class prep, when I get an email:

From: Jerome Tuggle (jtugg@gmail.com)
Subject: Short Story!! ;^)
Date: November 20, 2012 5:37:26 AM EST
To: Timbo (timboho007@bellsouth.net)

* *1 attachment (56kb)*

His dudeness:

Remember all those nights talking about fiction? And how I envied your ambition and talent? A dreamer no more: Believe it or don't, but I've finally managed to complete a short story with which I find satisfaction, so much so that I'm going to start sending it out (actually I already have). Hoping you'll give it a read-through to let me know what you think.

I'm experimenting on a few different levels, pushing things. Bear in mind too: this is the result of a bunch of prior attempts at this game, stuff nobody will see, mainly because I long got rid of it.

This one works, though. I think. In any case, Enjoy! LMK what you think. Of course YMMV.

—Tugg

PS: I let this guy post it on his blog—are you supposed to do that? If you're submitting it to magazines or journals? No comments from readers anyway, though.

http://wordpress.literarylionblog.com/wombat.html

I CLICK OPEN THE ATTACHMENT, a PDF. The title, mysterious, mammalian, a mouthful:

"NARCISSUS THE WOMBAT LOOKS WITHIN
AND SEES BUT A SAD RACCOON"
BY
JEROME TUGGLE
SHORT STORY
ABOUT 1976 WORDS

Well, if that title doesn't spark a reaction in an editor somewhere, I don't know what would. A little—precious, maybe.

Hrm.

Questions abound: A real wombat? From the wombat's POV?

Wombat as protagonist personified?

Allegory?

Children's fairy tale?

Both?

And what of the odd word count? Neither 'about 1900 words' nor the precise '1976 words,' but 'about' *a quite specified length* of 1976 words. Paradoxical.

A numerological correlation comes to mind: the fact that Jerome—as well, it should be noted, as this humble narrator—were both born in the storied year of the nation's glorious and celebrated bicentennial. Fascinating. A key to the code, perhaps?

AFTER READING THE STORY, I bang out a reply:

From: Tim Latham (timboho007@bellsouth.net)
Subject: re: Short Story!! ;^)
Date: November 20, 2012 10:40:17 am EST
To: The Tuggle (jtugg@gmail.com)

Tugg:

Good job. The title certainly grabbed me, and then the serious tone of the underlying piece quelled what concerns I had due to what I feared might be an indicator of preciousness, what with the woods-creatures and all. Habits of the wombat were interesting metaphors, though.

I can see how you were inspired to write this after the breakup with Monique last year—the long walks you took to clear your soul, as you put it. Into the woods. Staring into the mirrored lake. Said you'd had something revealed about yourself. All good, all depicted with the right degree of both distance as well as interior landscape.

Which leads me to what little criticism I have. While the language soars, we never make it outside of the narrator's erudite head. Where is the single scene necessary bet. the narrator and his "vanquished queen, undone by hubris that flowed both ways like [the?-must be a typo] schizophrenic, undulating waveform of a mountain stream"? We risk denying the reader the opportunity to judge matters for themselves through the revelatory nature of dialogue bet. characters rather than reportage.

Did this issue take away from my enjoyment of the piece? Not too much. I'd consider this mild criticism before trying to send it out—you'll get a barrage of "telling not showing" notes on your rejection slips (if you're lucky to get a note at all, of course! Bastards!! ☺).

Trust me—my students suffer this fusillade of wearying criticism on a weekly basis, but the hope is that they'll be all the better writers for having considered my words. May you do the same.

—Tim

PS Of course maybe you intended your narrator to be as isolated as he comes off, so in that case feel free to indeed approach my review with a grapefruit-sized grain of YMMV!!

I FIGURE, Tugg won't mind me being honest with him. Only way to improve. Criticism—it's the only thing that helps you help the material.

So, I hit *send*, move on to the next email; the next student's terrible paper. I'm working these days as a community college adjunct professor to supplement my freelance income, and this year in addition to the Fiction Workshop I & II and Creative Nonfiction, they've got me teaching the freshman section of good old American Lit. The semester wanes. Papers, piling up, and on. Have I become more teacher than writer?

But all I can do is keep thinking about the stories I've written, especially the unpublished ones, in which I tried to do what Tugg's up to in his, which is finding allegory in the mundanities of modern American life: a breakup with a girlfriend? Seemingly prosaic fodder for heady fiction, though when considered from the standpoint of near universal commonality—who hasn't suffered heartbreak?—the subject feels a sound one. All in the execution, which is solid. At least. Have to hope that Tugg takes my critique in the spirit that it's been offered. What do I know anyway? Only one person's asshole-slash-opinion.

"Tugg sent a story," I tell Becca over chips, salsa, and guac: That's right, it's Mexican night at Chateau Latham. We replicate a weekly pattern of meals which in its routine reminds me of how mama would always make pork chops on Mondays and fried chicken on Fridays.

"And?"

"Not bad." Crunch-crunch-crunch, spraying crumbs, a Brad Pitt impression. "Thought it could use another pass."

"Another what?"

A swig of microbrew. "Another revision."

"You criticized it?" Crunch-crunch. "Pass me the wine, please."

"Nah. Said it was good. A bit too much telling instead of showing."

"Ah-ha," a familiar criticism recognized. "That's a no-no."

"Yup. Did you know wombat feces come out square?"

"Ex-*cuse* me?"

"Some evolutionary bit of business . . .? They do it to mark their territory."

"What kind of story is this, anyway?"

"Well—a *really* personal one, actually."

She gives me a look: *Quit bullshitting*. "Starring a wombat? Better pass the wine."

Becca also teaches, heading up the English department at a private school in the Hamilton Hills neighborhood. Top money for K-12—she makes twice as much scratch as me, over which I'm neither emasculated nor challenged, only grateful in that release-of-breath way freelancers feel when the check from the regional small press magazine clears. We met in grad school, at Southeastern University. Actually, in a bar down in the Old Market. She was dating the bartender.

She pours and sips. "Did Tugg write fiction when y'all were roommates?"

"No, it's a more recent affectation."

"Thought so."

"Always a big reader, though. Sort-of the foundation of our friendship. The bookworm buddies. That's what the crew at Stendall," our dorm building, "called us."

"A regular comedy team, I'll bet."

"More like, quiet as a library in that room, usually."

Jerome works now at a top firm in Atlanta handling a single major international corporate client; my boy made good. One supposes.

His occasional emails ponder, sometimes, the emptiness of it all—a busy life has rendered the Tugg a lonesome vessel. Not hard to fathom how the Monique blowup must have been a major setback.

In the spirit of write-what-you-know, through this personal prism I see the bleak events of his 'fictional' story as a telling look into the mind of a person at a crossroads, uncertain of how and where and why to proceed, and indeed looking interrogatively within only to see the proverbial abyss —opaque, cold, soulless—staring back from pools of water encountered in three key locations: a grassy field by a nursing home, the asphalt parking lot of a liquor store, and then in a forest, the narrator watching as a raccoon drinks of the water of life from a placid, mirrored pond. The images of the glade, described like a cinematographer's dream Magic Hour shot, resonate and seem to symbolize a kind of nourishing rebirth following the hollow loneliness of the breakup. The narrator as wombat, photographed by Terrence Malick.

But he simply doesn't interact with anyone—the narrator, not the raccoon. That is. This narrator-as-human-wombat.

Ah-ha—the problem with the story.

The editor in me comes alive: Why not anthropomorphize the raccoon, have the entities dialogue with one another? My reasoning: If we're going to be denied an actual scene between the narrator and the lightly fictionalized, ethereal 'Monica,' then a discussion between wombat-man and actual woodlands creature, this could provide the spark the story needs. A suggestion, perhaps, to offer in a subsequent email. Assuming he takes the initial reply well enough to warrant such a further exchange.

Going into the study after dinner, a last swig of a good, heavy Argentinian red wine swirling in the balloon glass. Checking email. And there we have it, a fast-turnaround response from Tugg:

From: Jerome Tuggle (jtugg@gmail.com)
Subject: re: re: Short Story!! ;^)
Date: November 20, 2012 8:56:01 PM EST
To: Timbo (timboho007@bellsouth.net)

Good words, my friend. The solipsistic feel is indeed meant as a stylistic conceit, hence the lack of dialogue scenes bet. narrator and anyone else. Appreciate the feedback!

Best,
    Tugg

Ah, marvelous—he's gotten the thick skin about criticism. A no-biggie 'thanks' note rather than defensiveness. I raise my glass to Tugg.

Instead of hitting reply to offer up the more detailed critique I've concocted, I scroll through the body of the previous email and link over to the blogosphere version of Tugg's story. Skim through the web-formatted version.

Huh—doing so actually changes the feel of the story to me, makes it even more bleak and stark and filled with loneliness, those isolated chunks of paragraph, that rounded Helvetica typeface, the borders and sidebars further sequestering my friend's bitter words into units cut off not only from each other but also the outside world, unable to reach across the divide and click on a link to escape as I and everyone else may so easily do, a metaphor like the story itself: trapped by circumstance, unable to look outside the reality bubble of the broken romantic relationship.

But still. A little distancing and unsatisfying. All in the head. *Hrm.*

I make a post in the comments section, the first reader to do so. Initially I paste in my remarks from the private email, though with some revisions, like a summary statement that goes, *A few things I'd do differently, but overall the piece is pretty all right yadda yadda.*

Then, I add my Big Idea:

You could, of course, have the raccoon dialogue with the narrator, to further explicate his sense of isolation: only an animal will give him the time of day, that kind of thing. But in general, a good job, Mr. Tuggle! Keep up the strong writing.

I smile and hit *Post Comment.* Not a second thought about doing so... after all, I'm only trying to help.

THANKSGIVING COMES AND GOES, and now the homestretch for papers and pages in the classes. Yawning at the end of a blurry-eyed day of grading, I read through the last of the American Lit papers, this one about the Poe story 'The

Tarn' wherein the astute student correctly (in my opinion) posits that the 'tarn' or small lake of the title exists as a symbol for Poe's own real life substance abuse, issues with alcohol often being connected in dreams and stories with water imagery. Spot on, thinks me. *A*, the sage professor scratches in purple ink. Grading an A feels good. Rare creatures. Do kids read anymore?

Isn't staring at the smart-screened device reading? Huh? Aren't comment threads and text messages reading? Maybe the new standards aren't so much emerging as they're-here.

And then, I've had enough of reading. What I ought to do, I think, is go home and work on a few short story submissions of my own, or that unfinished magazine feature which might actually return income. But, too beat. Life, getting in the way.

Wondering, then, about Tugg and his Wombat. If he went ahead and sent out the piece.

BUSY FOR WEEKS, then away over the holidays at Becca's family's place in Connecticut, a few trips into the city for a Broadway show and an evening out, then back home to the temperate southland for a few days of housekeeping before a new semester starts.

Before I know it, the short, frigid days lengthen, and it's March. A warming trend, a surprise cold snap, but a week later, the first blush of wet and crisp, true springtime. Elmore Leonard says you shouldn't describe the weather unless it has a direct bearing on the story, so let me add that the clean and fresh air matches my mood, as I've set out to finally complete a second novel over the coming summer. At last. The first had been at twenty-six. A long time ago. Resting comfortably in the trunk, to stay.

Already underway during the spring term on pre-writing, I spend many hours doing character background and research and note-taking and daydreaming. Becca says it appears that more than half of the writer's work seems to be done lying on the couch or pacing around staring off into space. That maybe we're putting one over on the rest of the world. That ain't working, she jokes.

Is too, I reply—that's the way you do it. So long as you also write a little.

ONE EVENING I'm up late querying the local alt weekly on a feature article I've written about a homegrown, troubadour musician who came to the trade late in life after following a career in law, musicians being his heroes and idols and playing music having been his lifelong dream. Which is not unlike my buddy Jerome Tuggle and writing fiction.

The analogy jogs the realization that I haven't heard from my old roommate in several months now, not since the short story email exchange. And my blog post comment.

Not even a holiday card last year.

Huh.

Like I said before, drifting apart. College, ages ago now. Forty, soon.

SOMETIME AROUND SPRING BREAK, I get a terse note from Tugg telling me he's coming to town to meet with some other corporate lawyering types about a bit of arcane lawyering business. I am delighted to respond by offering an evening out on the Latham tab, conclude by asking how the writing's going. If he'd sent out 'Wombat' like he'd planned, et cetera.

No reply. Busy lawyer, after all. Probably has no time for these personal relationships.

Maybe some insight there.

A week later, right after we've cleared away the brunch dishes and gotten the laundry going, we get a phone call that interrupts this blessed Sunday afternoon ritual—next will be a trip to the grocer, then the preparation of food for the coming week so that neither of us has to kill ourselves getting lunches and dinners together for us and the kid; we're organized, a method to our day of biblically-mandated 'rest, chores, planning, list making. Life. But a routine disrupted, as the call's from Tugg. Who's now here in town—I've forgotten about his visit.

"My man, here at last. Where you at?" An old joke: the learned college men using bad grammar.

He tells me. Says, come on out. First round's on me.

I head over that way. Back-pounding man hugs.

In the hotel lobby of the new high rise Sheraton downtown, he reports that the rooftop bar's packed with laminate-draped conventioneers. Instead, he suggests, we cruise down near campus to the old haunts—the ones I still haunt, as it were, being a hometown boy who successfully resisted the tug and pull of the young man's call to adventure.

The urge to roam, suppressed. We married young. Too young. Kids. It happens; it's all-good.

We pause long enough for a selfie taken against the cool white winter sunset. Our faces, wide and pink, the downtown skyline falling away from us to either side. Big smiles, arms draped.

"One more," Tugg says. "But serious faces."

"Writer faces?"

A shadow across his face, a faltering of the smile. "Sure."

That one, dramatic and dark. Something about not smiling makes my age more apparent. The gray in my goatee. Writerly enough, one supposes. Tugg looks like the serious person he is even when not smiling, however, and I tell him so, and he seems to appreciate this with a quiet nod on the brief elevator ride to the street and a cab that sits, seemingly waiting for us.

The Parlor's a classy, dark, grownup joint amidst the rest of the beer bars in the college ghetto a few blocks from campus. It opens every day at three, even Sunday, the slow day for them—they don't have blaring HD TV sets on every wall with NASCAR or football or the sporting event du jour, only quiet jazz played live on weekend nights, but mostly courtesy the satellite radio station that never stops, flowing with smooth jazz tunes. The Parlor: a hip room—a writer's room.

Tugg looks good, tanned, trim, an affront to my softening body and dimpled skin stretched taut beneath a low thread-count T-shirt, one of a three-pack I'd gotten on sale at Target. Settled into a corner table, Tugg orders a couple of microbrews, hoppy as hell. Nothing like the cheap crap we used to lug by the case up to the dorm room.

We clink glasses. "Has it been, what, five years now? A travesty."

"Time's getting slippery."

"True enough. Starting to think I'm never gonna get that big novel underway."

"Mm-hm."

He sips his foamy bev, catches me up on all things Tugg: Work stuff that's keeping him in and out of that hellish ATL airport. The Monique aftermath; a brief, hopeless dalliance with a woman much younger. Months later the hint of a whiff of a chance of a reconciliation with Monique, but the perceived opportunity squelched and nullified by the sad truth that her only real desire had been to recover property left behind in Jerome's stunning downtown condo.

It's perfect for a bachelor like him, he's told me. Views north and west, amazing sunsets, romantic.

"So how's the writing going," I hear myself ask through a warm, bubbling eructation. "Cranking it out?"

Tugg shrugs. "Pretty okay, I guess."

"What about the Wombat? Any luck placing it?"

He takes a long time to answer. Blooms of pink form in his cheeks, an alcohol flush. "Well. It's like this."

In measured and even tones, he relates how much my blog comments had wounded him. How arrogant I'd come off. How the post almost, *almost* derailed an acceptance from a small journal. How my friend had stewed and simmered for all these months over my alleged transgression.

To my relief, however, came an epilogue as I sat mute: everything worked out, and the story would be published in a few months; a personal triumph for him.

"The most meaningful moment of my adult life."

Eek. "But look—the blog post comment. It was just the same feedback I'd emailed to you."

Now he lets his true anger be shown—a serious face for sure. "'I'd have done a few things differently?' Listen to how that sounds. In any case, you planted a seed of doubt in that editor's head. 'Ya know, this dude's kinda right,' he says. 'Maybe you could have him talk to the raccoon'."

"Shit."

"Jesus. *Jay-sus*, Timbo."

"Party foul?"

"You putz."

I beg again that the remark was intended as innocuous summation, one meant with neither hubristic intent nor definitude, a word Becca and I made up a few years ago to describe George W. Bush's depth of certainty in areas like foreign policy and war-making. "Only wanted to help."

"You almost effed up my first, at long-last, mother-effing fiction publication credit."

"There's more than one way to write, that's all I meant. Not right and wrong... I'd have done it differently. I am me. You are you. But hey. So long as it works."

"Somebody thinks so, anyway."

"Touché."

"And stop explaining yourself."

He doesn't ask me what I've been writing, which is fine. Nothing much to report, honestly. The short story well, dry for over a year now. Longer. And the novel not yet underway. Pre-writing, though, sounds too mincing and mealy-mouthed to verbalize.

Some of the tension discharged, conversation turns instead to the old days—romps, parties, girls, memories.

Says he hasn't given up on finding another Monique; implies but doesn't so much say that he envies me—my life, my wife. Thinks this time he got close, but no cigar.

Sloshing, dyspeptic, outside on the sidewalk. "Probably time for a—*hup*—meal."

I agree. "Speaking of the better half, let's call and get her down here. Maybe the Indian joint. Whatever you've got a taste for."

"Sounds great. Let's do that."

Sentiment washes over him. Hugs me standing in the median.

"Ah," Tugg says. "Damn fine to be here with you."

"Same here."

His face looks more youthful now, the old Jerome peeking through the grownup crust of Tugg the lawyer, Tugg the aggrieved petitioner for redress of grievances, in this case for the dignity he'd seen as disparaged by my blog posting: His eyes now crinkled and kind, his spirit unburdened, the head of indignant steam now dissipated.

And me? As proud of him as I'd been once I first heard that he'd decided to try his hand at fiction.

So I'd had some reservations about the work; sue me. As the comedian punch-lined, I may not know much about art, but I know what I like.

When it comes to friendship, however? I don't know so much what I like, but what I need. And it's more important than literary criticism. That's for damn sure.

release into prayer

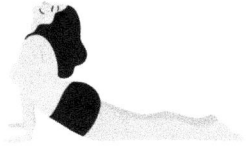

AWAKENING FROM A SHALLOW DREAM IN WHICH SHE felt herself flying in a different way, flung laughing into the air by a smelly old biker friend of her Uncle Junior's over thirty years ago, Lucy Latham grips the armrest on the flight from LaGuardia to Charlotte, a half-empty, ghostly aluminum tube hurtling through the cold night air. A high, persistent whistle, at the threshold of perception, bleeds in from outside the Airbus, a sound effect ill-befitting engines of such stupendous, thrumming power—power enough to hold these souls aloft, Lucy and her airborne brethren. So that they will all arrive alive. How important it must feel to be a pilot.

An emergency, drop-everything trip back home: a father taken ill, sudden, and despite her haste, still possibly too late to experience a mutual goodbye. Once upon a time, Lucy had never wanted to speak with him again, but now, finality compelled her to seek out some version of a last word. Perhaps only to have the last word. From the anguished sound of Timmy's voice, she'd indeed get the last word. For a change.

She never became an adult in her father's eyes. Whether

the art or the yoga, he never approved. The real crime had been leaving Edgewater County, and South Carolina altogether.

A choking sob, one kept to herself so as not to attract the attention of the corpulent, besuited business-type across the aisle: fleshy jowls hanging over an open collar, an incarnadine drunk's nose buried in a Tom Clancy potboiler (with some co-writer, of course, a brand more than a true novelist) grabbed from the newsstand racks. Imbibing her own drink, a second glass of cheap white wine like cold vinegar, nonetheless sliding down with the ease of spring water. Trying to read a magazine while bouncing around on the approach, her stomach sloshing. The words on the glossy pages were only a messy, incoherent jumble.

Lucy, alone. On the plane, in her daily life. Surrounded by people—friends, students, and the general hubbub of urban humanity—a strawberry blonde yoga beast, yet a solitary one. And soon fatherless as well. Would she miss this crucial life connection, even a major one like that of the Latham patriarch? TBD—she hadn't gone home for several holiday seasons now. Who knew why; her reasons had been mere excuses. Timmy, always there, now living back in the county himself. It's fine. It's all fine.

LUCY. Or rather, Sissy, as designated first by her parents, and later by pundits like the casual set of creative class types who make up Lucy's social circle, key members of which she met through the yoga classes she teaches since the art thing didn't —hasn't—worked out. Making enough to live in the city, in Brooklyn. Barely.

Thanking god for yoga. Every day. And meaning it—

having the glow. They weren't kidding about that core-building being a spiritual one, in addition to the hard abs and lean flesh.

Earlier that morning, she'd taught one class before getting the call about her father. "Toned and owned, baby—that's what you want." Her catch phrase, the booster, the pep talk, the you-are-going-to-look-and-feel-so-good prodding necessary to get her charges through the more strenuous poses; it didn't have to actually make sense.

Sweat dripping onto mats; groans. "Do the best you can," she prompted them. "Getting better, always. That's the key. That's the growth. That's the exercise. That's the benefit."

Mr. Cohen—50s, bookish, his back tender from an injury—got stuck in a down-dog. "Ah, hell," falling to one knee. "Not so toned, but maybe owned."

Lucy brought the class out of the full sun salutation, releasing into prayer, with glorious deep breaths and gratified, or else grimaced, upturned faces. Praising, offering positive reinforcement in her chipper, soothing voice. "Don't be discouraged. You're getting better all the time. Stronger, better balance. Balance in yoga is *everything*..."

Cohen eases up from his knees and prepares for the next series of poses. "You make it look so easy."

Impish. "Um—that's why I'm the instructor."

"Touché."

"Look at it this way: if the poses were easy," breathing in long and deep, raising her lean arms to the ceiling of the studio, in midtown on the second floor, the retail level, of a glimmering condo tower of glass and steel, "there'd be no point to this activity. And when they do get easy, then we—"

"—*step it up*," as several voices, veterans of her classes, completed the thought. Beaming at them, she agrees and praises her adepts.

Lucy, in possession of a body indeed in some measure of peak condition, marred only by a creeping layer of padding around the hips. Wine, the principal culprit; going out three or four nights a week, with friends, on dates, socializing. Her peeps. Best as she could tell. Filling a void, she supposes.

Upon landing in Charlotte, a shock: Cold, deep bone-chilling winter cold, the icy wind hurting her exposed ears, her coat far too thin—WTF? What had happened to her sunny south? She'd always had low body fat, felt sensitive to drops in temperature, as in a hot and heavy relationship, one you'd thought serious, that suddenly cools, as with her last beau. A cold that gets into the bones.

Her brother, Timmy, pulls up to the curbside. Hugging, holding one another.

"I could've just rented a car. I hate being picked up like I'm nine years old."

Dismissive. "Forget about it. I needed to get out of that hospital anyway. He's been—it's been a long night and day." Timmy manhandles her duffle bag into the vehicle, not meeting her eyes. "It could be weeks, they're saying now."

"*Weeks*—that's not what you said on the phone! I can't stay here for weeks."

Finally looking at her, he shrugs. "It's not what I knew at the time. I dunno what to tell ya."

Driving, grinding their way south through godawful I-77 traffic in silence, a knot of red taillights and blinkers and rain and cars sliding and changing lanes, four lanes, three, until finally, entering good old South Carolina: passing Rock Hill and along the now-rural freeway, twenty minutes until the turnoff, and here, Edgewater County.

Lucy, sighing, shivering, holding her pale frozen hands in front of the warm vents. "What about this changing prognosis?"

"About Dad?"

Sarcastic, bilious. "*Who else*? Jesus."

Timmy looks like a man holding his breath, his shoulders hunched, hands gripping the wheel at ten and two o'clock. Asks what does he look like, a doctor? "Daddy's not awake. All I can tell you."

His accent sounds so pronounced compared to hers. She flattened it out. Or living up 'yonder' did. Her last boyfriend said that, when she called home to talk to her father, her voice sounded different, softer and more Southern. An unconscious habit, she reckons.

Lucy scoffs, shakes her head. "I'm just asking for information."

The two discuss in sober and solemn terms their father's condition, their speech colored by fatigue and pessimism as well as sibling rancor, a holdover from a contentious shared childhood composed of various emotionally scarring events. Scattered kid's toys and soda-pop stains decorate the cloth seats of the purring, warm SUV: Timmy, a family man for years now, married young to a girl he met at Southeastern University, a daughter, doing well; Timmy, a creative adman with awards and thinking of writing books one day, and the wife an English teacher. Good match. "So wholesome and healthy and by-the-numbers it makes you want to go out a fucking window," as Lucy characterizes her brother's life to her hipster friends back home in Brooklyn. She lives without a roommate in a 750 square foot rent-controlled flat in Greenpoint right off McCarren Park, and takes the New York Subway G-line only a few minutes to her job in Manhattan. Has a tree-lined street that helps with having been a country mouse now living in the vast and unforgiving Sodom of concrete and steel.

Timmy, exiting the freeway, asks a familiar question. "So, are you dating?"

"Yes and no."

"Come on, Sissy..."

"That's the best answer I can give you."

"Is you or ain't you?"

Lucy, sighing, tracing a finger in the condensation on the window, a sideways figure 8. "No one seriously."

"Are you ever going to date anyone seriously?"

"What, is it like turning on a switch? I can't find the right one. Yet."

"*In all of New York City?*" Timmy, always a bit of an uptight, smarmy know-it-all. "You're a decent enough looker. You must be doing something wrong."

More sarcasm, a knife-edge. "You'd know. You and dad've always made sure to point out everything I've ever done wrong, usually even before I did it."

"Sissy... really? Not now."

You're just not used to being the baby of the family, and treated that way too, but of course he's right; now, not the time to re-litigate old cases.

IN THE ICU waiting room are family members, many not seen in years. Small talk, catching up, piteous looks, remembrances of the prior Latham tragedy—her mother, dead from a virulent and sudden cancer back when Lucy'd been but an ingenue, a college freshman, now long in the past. So many people she knew from around Chilton and that part of Edgewater County had gotten cancer. That damned nuclear station on the river. Had to be.

Dad, in the interim since then remarrying not once but twice, though neither subsequent wife, Lucy notes with acerbic and pitiless judgment, appears to be in attendance. Timmy explains his spouse, Becca—a claustrophobic person—found herself simply too uncomfortable to stay in the waiting room. Instead, she's off helping with their youngest, remaining at home to await news.

The prognosis, what few details available, is indeed not good: Dad, the victim of a serious MI event, with many hours passing before being discovered. Now lying comatose, with difficulty ascertaining his future condition upon a presumed, eventual reawakening. Hope, at this point, came at a premium.

The doctor, lacking a sunny disposition—his demeanor runs the wide-ranging gamut from taciturn to matter-of-fact—says like a monotone robot, "He's stable. We're doing—um. All we can for him. But at this point? We—um. Simply can't say. What's to come."

Timmy, exhausted and snappish. "You'd better make damn sure you're doing enough."

The doctor frowned. "We'll do nothing less than everything we can, Mr. Latham. Tonight will tell the tale, really. Tonight. And maybe—tomorrow."

The little pause spoke volumes about her father's chances.3

In the corridor Lucy breaks down, is comforted by a cousin proffering tissues and a shoulder on which to lean. Lucy, ashamed, feeling weak, waving distant relative off, declaring herself all right. Reigning in her tears:

Her father, forbidding the leaking of eyes.

Rules.

Expectations.

Hanging over her head, a purple smudge of a cloud, a pop-up summer thundershower like back home. Home, yes: Brooklyn, not here. Here, no longer home.

Not even the old lake house, going back in the family to Dad's granddad, and oh! how she'd loved it there as a girl. The last visit there'd been for a cousin's wedding, and Lucy's time had been spent wandering along the lakeshore with a sketchpad and iPod, crushed by bittersweet song lyrics.

Avoiding the questions from family members back then, too:

Career?

Men?

Your degree?

Your art—what happened with all that?

An uncle speculating how difficult, surely, to make a decent living as a yoga instructor. Lucy, disabusing such notions: teaching classes every day at the studio, but also picking up extra work: the Senior Center, a hospital's employee fitness program. Living modestly, not getting rich, but wealth not the point. Fitness and good health, for herself, and giving some back to the community at large. Noble.

A hospital restroom stinks of someone's furtive cigarette fix; a mirror reveals a disheveled wreck of a face. Freshening up, then coming back down the sterile corridor, Lucy wishes to vanish.

At the sight of an aged, familiar face, however, she brightens: A beloved aunt on her father's side, Penny.

Sad, dewy eyes, fleshy arms hugging her; reaching up, holding Lucy's face in warm powder-dry hands. "I always forget how tall you got. But no matter, you'll always be little Sissy to me." Looking her up and down. "Darling—you're so thin. Are you well?"

Lucy, thinking that, other than the wine layer as she considers her modest hip padding, she stands before Aunt Penny in the unequivocal best shape of her life. "It's the yoga."

Aunt Penny, squinting, a hearing aid, leaning in. "You're eating yogurt?"

"Yeah," laughing. "That's it. No—my job. I teach yoga."

"Well now, don't overdo it. There's such a thing as *too* skinny."

"Let's split the difference and call it 'lean.'"

"That's fine, dear."

They stroll back toward the ICU waiting room. "So Dad's really done it this time, eh?"

Aunt Penny, ignoring the crisis at hand, returns to the question of physique. "Here's what we need—let's get a juicy ribeye in you, a baked potato, some good-old starchy home cooking. A hot, goopy mac and cheese like Mee-maw used to make. Oh, how I miss those summertime cookouts at the lake house. Those were the fun years—when you all were still little."

Fading memories: Timmy and Lucy, a smattering of cousins, friends, always a passel of house apes running around, baseball games and croquet on the big grassy lawn in the summer, fishing in the cove, Timmy floating around in his little johnboat. It'd all ended, it seemed, so suddenly. It'd never been the same after Mama died. And Lucy, only years later realizing how easily she succumbed to anxiety must surely be related to having been at hand for her grandmother's heart attack. She'd done it without therapy, too. Couldn't afford it.

"Those were such happy times. I miss them."

"One day when you have your own babies, you'll have it

again." Canting her head. "When *are* you going to find your special someone?"

Lucy, examining the tips of her sneakers, drew in a long breath. "It's not a priority."

"Pish-posh." Aunt Penny, reddening. "And let me, let me just say," lowering her voice, "if it's *Miss* Right you're looking for, well—I think that's *fine*, just fine. It's—fine, darling."

Lucy, assuring her aunt it wasn't that—lord, but if it were? No prob, not in her artsy crowd.

Considering the idea of kids and family, of settling down, Lucy thinks of her hipster boho crowd back in Brooklyn, none of them truly successful at artistic ventures, all working day jobs, many of which were in the service industry; most of her friends younger by a few years than her, one or two older, and yet, despite their own setbacks and heartbreaks and epic fails, outwardly less bitter than the way she often feels. Within this group are only childless couples and one marriage, between a would-be scribe writing novels while working as a reporter and movie reviewer for an alt weekly, with his bride a poet forever chipping away at a dissertation she struggled to crack: Dean and Nance. Seeming in deep love; perfect for each other. They sit in tandem at desks in the same room and write at the same time.

Aw. Lucy, an ache at such intimacy, which to her came only as a fantasy.

But not for lack of effort: Lucy, dating one or two out of this group of folks who spend their evenings hanging around the coffee shops and bars and bistros in Williamsburg, the clubs and galleries and downtown and the clubs. Dating, screwing, getting nowhere. Desperate for intimacy, but for all her good health and decent looks finding none, none beyond explosive but ephemeral physicality. Guy she'd dated for two months—an eternity by her standards—split the scene saying he couldn't get inside her head. After two months? she thought. Everybody so impatient anymore.

Her, no different. Wanting the spark, never feeling it. Pretending to feel it. But it's not there, the voice in her head sounding like George Carlin, mugging and shaking his head at the audience. *You're lookin' for it, kid. But it-ain't-here.*

A portrait of desperation—going so far as to try a dating service. Disaster. An all-but, next-thing feeling like organized prostitution, this dumpy balding cat showing up nervous and acting like a john, also looking very little like his photo-shopped profile pic. Running lines on her. Talking and flirting over glasses of Pinot Noir and making remarks and insinuations and icky, obvious euphemisms.

Have another drink, he said. "It's on me," with an unsubtle leer. "On me," he repeated. "Anywhere on me. If you want."

Thinking indeed about dumping the wine all over him. Not going home with that one, no, and canceling her listing on the service.

INSISTING that she stay so Timmy could get rest, Lucy—Sissy—curls up in a hospital chair with a blanket procured from one of the LPNs.

A long night. Nurses in and out, but no change; nothing to check, nothing to report.

The next morning, Timmy returns in time for the lead doctor to take the siblings aside, his expression flat but for the downturned mouth, Lucy thinks, of the grim messenger he presents rather than as healer.

News, worse; Dad, fading, not coming back.

At least he'd left the decision to the documents and not

his kids, she thinks. Not that she would have struggled with the decision. She feels as emotionless as Spock delivering routine scanning results to William Shatner sitting in his command seat, legs crossed and fingertips touching. Objective and dispassionate; just the facts.

The time is measured in hours. Her father's breathing grows heavy and infrequent. No opportunities for words, final or otherwise.

Hating herself. Thinking, *Damn you*, unsure if she means herself or her father. She puts her face in her hands, but she doesn't cry.

Huh, he says, finally. And goes away. A farewell, a death rattle.

Timmy, a blubbering wreck, wishes to stay in the room with the body for an indeterminate amount of time; Lucy, offering to deal with the arrangements as a way of hightailing her way out of there, as though the devil at the heels of her sneakers, the comfy casual shoes she chose for the plane ride. A body. Not her father. Whatever he had been, had gone.

A WHIRLWIND. Funerary bits of business. Assessing the contents of the house, the clothing.

All of it caused a reversal from before: Now Timmy, eyes dry, takes charge from Lucy, a crumbly, weepy mess.

Edgewater County—ugh. It had gotten to her.

A difficult scene: the meeting with the pastor, the Reverend Duson Mire of the First Baptist Church of Chilton, to discuss the eulogy. His coat seems too small. Pastors in a place like Edgewater County are well fed.

"In terms of his memorial, tell me what you'll remember most about him, any stories that typify either how we'd like to remember him," the Rev suggests in helpful measured tones, with a gentle, warm smile; the use of the royal We, she knows, is a sign of solidarity, the survivors shouldering together as a bulwark against the howling void of evermore that'd taken the elder Latham at the too-young age of sixty-four, his 'whole retirement' robbed from him as Timmy keeps expressing in hushed, tragic whispers. "Or how we feel he might best wish to be remembered. Milestones in his life. Accomplishments—Timmy's already given me a laundry list, so that part will come easily and naturally, and of course I knew him from his civic activities in Edgewater County. A wonderful man, your father. Wonderful, wonderful. We're all just so so sorry."

Lucy, a short barking laugh, *yap yap*. "I want him to be remembered best as his father's daughter... I mean, his daughter's father." Not so much crumbling now as near-giddy. Laughing and slapping her knee. "Or, as a great general commanding troops in the field. A mentor. A man's man." Outright cackling. Unable to bottle up the ill-defined anger any longer, the emotion released as mad merriment. "A man among men. A behemoth among giants, astride the shores of Lake Hollings like Paul Bunyon looking west, looking for his blue ox..." She's barely able to breathe. "A saint. A fucking saint."

"Gracious. I see, I see. Yes yes, my dear."

Timmy's face, the color of a brick. "*Sissy*! What's got into you?"

She collects herself. "A man for whom his greatest accomplishment, perhaps, was *always* telling his daughter how wonderful she was." Laughter again, but turning to tears, a torrent, her head spinning. Lucy, pushing away at Timmy, who reaches over to comfort her. Through blurry vision, seeing the Reverend Mire give her red-faced brother a be-patient hand signal, a tiny fluttering of fingertips, the shooing away of concern: *This is normal.*

"I'm fine," she says through a froggy throat. "I apologize—for the tone of—all that."

The men, discussing matters, while Lucy sits awash in bitter remembrance: after the cancer diagnosis—far along, metastasized—how she'd dropped out of college to be with her ailing mother. Lucy, maintaining courage for months, the strong one for her brother and her father and her mother, too.

Surgeries; one three-hour procedure ending up lasting ten. Timmy a wreck, Lucy in control. Preparing for that particular funeral by being a rock, a decision maker, level-headed. Brave for her mother, brave for them all. Picking out the casket, floral arrangements, music. All with Mom still breathing, still living, a wraith, a bag of bones, body mass negligible—near the end, nineteen year-old Lucy was able to lift her own mother up off the sheet, the woman but a shell, a rag doll of papery skin sewn over a frame of insubstantial balsa. Afraid she'd break the body from which Lucy had come.

"Timothy, what about you? Tell me about your dad."

"Yes," Lucy says in a steady voice, recovered from her crying jag. "Do tell, Timmy—you were his favorite, after all."

Timmy, daggers for eyes. "He was a great father to *both* of us. That's how he's going to be remembered." Definitive. "Father, husband. Businessman. A pillar of his community."

That much, true; Dad, a Rotarian, a participant in municipal government by sitting on various committees, an active letter-writer to the *Edgewater Advocate*—in Lucy's childhood, her father had been but a grocery store manager, but he'd gone to night school at Piedmont Tech and gotten a certificate and started an electrical business, one that he sold only just last year and from which he'd only recently retired. He'd been able to pay every dime of Lucy and Timmy's college without taking a loan. It'd been so much cheaper back then, the early 80s. Under a grand for a semester at Southeastern. Unbelievable. Lucy, glad she didn't have to worry about a college fund for some squalling rugrat.

Lucy, settling down and trying to be serious. Now allowing Timmy to do all the talking, letting him indeed decide how the local historians were to define the great Mr. Latham at his public remembrance. Timmy, the pastor, their voices becoming murky like the teacher in a *Charlie Brown* animated half-hour.

A certain shock settled in, finally. The century, ending this year. And daddy... dead.

TWO DAYS LATER, on the way to the funeral, Aunt Penny offers her a Xanax. Lucy, not a pill-taker by nature, but accepting the oval pill anyway; dry-swallowing, feeling the medication stick in her craw. Halfway through the service, a pervasive sense of unreality takes hold, of stepping outside herself the way people say they feel during near-death experiences.

The rest, a blur.

Until... Mitch.

Graveside. A man comes up to her, handsome, familiar.

Lucy, eyes crossing from the pill, in a fog, manages to focus on a set of green-gray peepers, and catching her breath at the realization: Mitch Colcannon, a high school friend, but more than that—a raging crush, ever unrequited. How the adolescent Lucy had wished for more than friendship but had never been approached by him, not in that way. Nor doing any Sadie Hawkins asking of her own. Mitch: quiet, studious, fit, a baseball player but not one of the dumb jock types—a catch.

Sweet Mitch—always warm, charming, cordial and never, ever available. If she recalled correctly, he'd had two longterm childhood girlfriends, one right after another—eighth grade through first half of tenth with cute blonde Natalie Kline, later with smoldering sexpot Karen Varga, hooking up a week after the breakup with Natalie and remaining attached at the hip right on through graduation. Lucy has perfect recall of these facts, much more so than most of what they'd been learning in class.

"Is that who I think it is?"

"Lucy...?" Hugging, tight, patting her on the back. "I'm so *so* sorry."

"It's okay. He didn't suffer." It strikes her: "How did you know him?"

"From the barber shop, mainly. Lord, but he could cut the fool with the best of them. Jokes like you never heard."

Lucy, stunned. It sounded like a different person from the more silent and serious father figure she knows.

Knew.

Mitch gave her a subtle once-over, his eyelashes fluttering. "Goodness—you haven't aged a minute."

Lucy, scanning for a ring, finding his hands barren of finger furniture. "Neither have you."

"What's the secret?"

Before she could answer, a buzzing phone inside his suit jacket pocket curtailed the conversation, while Lucy is pulled away by Timmy to continue the ungodly and endless acknowledgement of well-wishers and fellow mourners, cousins and acquaintances and a gray-haired woman, tearful, Lucy remembered as one of the check-out girls from the

Release into Prayer 171

Piggly Wiggly where her father worked when she had been a prepubescent.

Lucy, glancing over her black-clad shoulder for Mitch, but he's gone into the hubbub of folks making their way to the line of cars parked along the rutted tracks of the old cemetery. Lucy, convincing herself that seeing her old crush presented a good omen, but without a shred of confidence; panicking at the thought of not seeing him again. Of this being some cosmic meeting; how missing her chance would be a crime of almost spiritual implications. She has to act.

THE TRADITIONAL POST-FUNERAL GATHERING, held in this case not at the tiny old family home on the bend in the road, but at the beloved Latham family lake house: with the weight of the grim ceremonies in the past, a cacophony of voices, laughter, tears; old friends, cousins, uncles, aunts; it all came to her in a warm, comforting buzz.

Lucy, however, distinct and distracted, drifting around and swilling coffee; woozy, she remembers why she tends to eschew pharmacological palliatives like the pill her aunt proffered.

Looking around for Mitch, but not seeing him.

Pulling herself away, going outside, acknowledging a knot of smokers clustered against the chilly wind, which is nothing compared to a brutal January New York morning walking to the subway to go teach yoga. Lucy, not feeling the cold, the lake a finger of ripple-swept tarn reflecting back the ashen sky, shimmery slate gray, like her mood. As the song asks: *where on earth is the sun, anyway?*

Alone on the deck, she anticipates the coming song of nightbirds. Did the whippoorwills call out this time of year?

Tentative footfalls on the weathered decking behind her, a shuffle. Watching him approach her, she loses her breath. Butterflies in her belly, like she used to get in high school when a cute boy would talk to her.

"Hello again."

Collecting herself. "I didn't think you were coming."

His voice, small and sheepish. "Truthfully?"

She waits.

"I wanted to get caught up with you some more."

Playing it cool. "I'm glad. But I might be all out of small talk."

"Oh," dejected. "I'll let you be, then."

"No—I mean, with all those folks inside. Not you."

"Family can be exhausting, even in the best of times." A smile, one radiating good will. "Let's take a stroll, shall we?"

Lucy, offering her his arm, the two of them heading toward the water. Lucy, huddling against the wind, but not against him. Too soon.

LIKE THE LAKE, time now becomes liquid, transitory. The afternoon waning, winter light already soft now fading into darkness, when she should have been thinking of her father and the past all she sees is Mitch.

Old feelings, old regrets—some verbalized, others conveyed only by blushing cheeks or downcast eyes. Mitch. So warm and comforting and open to her complaints about life. Nodding. Not giving up too much about himself. Asking how so-and-so is. Who died. Who got married or divorced. Fourteen years since high school. Since band—so handsome, Mitch, playing the trumpet while she honked on the clarinet. Woodwind and brass. Two different sections.

During the reluctant, lingering farewell hug, Lucy wonders if Mitch can feel the need coming off her in waves, like rippling heat from a sun-struck strip of summer asphalt. How she would eat him alive tonight, if only she could get across.

A final thought, a serene expression spilling across his handsome face: "Lucy, it might not be any of my business—"

Lucy, anticipatory. *He's about to ask whether I'm attached, whether I'm seeing someone!* A new generation of butterflies, hatching inside her belly. "What?"

"—but if you haven't yet opened your heart to Jesus Christ, there's no better time than right now, at this moment of loss and confusion."

Taken aback. She didn't see this one coming. "Loss, yes. But confusion? Not so much. My mom died too young. Maybe I'm used to it."

"Not to be presumptuous... but what about faith?"

"Sure, faith, yes." She considered her commitment to yoga, and to meditation, except when she slept in and found herself running late. "I believe what I believe," which in an epiphany she now sees as not-much.

"Wonderful. A strong faith in God's the only way to realize your fullest potential, as well as make sure you'll have a place—you know, a *special* place—afterwards. Deciding how best to serve God. Eschewing temptations, and indulgences, and—trust me on this. It's a no-brainer."

Disappointment: Lucy, a person of spirit—how high the yoga makes her feel!—but not of faith, seeing now a major stumbling block to any ongoing relationship with this one. Feeling that to have thought so a sign of desperation anyway —a high school crush, for pity's sake. She needed to get over herself. "Thanks for spending time with me."

"A pleasure, and a *duty*." Mitch, touching her on the

sleeve: "Think about what I said. And consider getting out of the sinful old city 'up yonder.' This is God's country, right here in South Carolina..."

THE FLIGHT BACK HOME, an hour forty-five, two if against a headwind. An ache inside, but not over her father:

Scenarios of long distance romance playing like a movie in Lucy's head, the whistle of the engines not heard, the paperback in her lap going unread: Dating Mitch? How? The gulf of the miles presenting more of an immediate problem than the divergence in belief systems; yoga as her center, her Tao, her great spirit, not bearded men from somewhere beyond the wispy clouds outside the aircraft window, and certainly not the black-robes who insisted they stood as God's intermediary. Belief in living not for eternity, but for the moment at hand—the presence of mind which comes with yoga, along with the hot bod. So fulfilling.

Mitch, so sweet, kind, and handsome as the day is long, like always, the son of a bitch... Lucy, unable to get that face out of her mind.

Phone calls and emails began and continued with increasing frequency; her old crush so patient, so willing to listen. Nights once spent out with her crowd now tabled and put-off, instead alone at home tap-tapping on a social networking site, one she'd persuaded a reluctant Mitch to also join. Mitch, not giving up on her, occasionally exhorting the necessity of strong, bedrock faith in God, gentle reminders offered during their hours-long chat sessions.

Lucy, wondering if, in order to keep Mitch on the hook, she should feign belief. Belief in his unseen gods. Wondering if she could talk him into chat sex.

Lucy, so taken with Facebook chatting and messaging with Mitch she sometimes misses her stop and finds herself racing blocks back down Broadway to the studio.

Addicted to him.

Desperate for this to work out.

Mitch himself admitting a growing sense of affection for her, one beyond friendship.

But as he's beginning to ask, what would this involve, Mitch and Lucy? Relocation? By whom? To where?

Panic. Panic at moving back. Panic at this not working out.

Calling him. Eager to see him in person, almost frantic. Ringing. Ringing. Voice mail:

"*Hi, this is Mitch, I'm unable to get to you right now, so please leave a message and have a blessed day...*"

Neutral stammering pleasantries, then going for more, for broke. Fumbling, stumbling over her words. "I've decided something. You need to come and visit me." Face hot, throwing ideas out there, enticements. Making to ring off, adding in a blurted jumble: "Mitch, *I love you*."

Calling back that night, his voice came tentative and small, asking small-talky questions, going uh-huh, uh-huh.

Heart pounding, she finally asks, "So... what did you think about my idea?"

"I don't know how I can justify it."

"A little getaway to come and visit *moi*? Come on, it'll be fun. I'll show you the city. Can't promise a Broadway show, that's too trite. But something real New York-ish."

"I'm sure it'd be grand, Lucy. But... what is this?"

"It is what it is." An edge to her voice. "C'mon, why not?"

"I just... I enjoy this friendship of ours."

"Me too, honey."

"But I wonder where it's going." A beat. "Where it could go, I mean. The distance, and all."

"Distance can be fixed." Breathing hard, holding the handset away, not wanting him to think her sounding like an obscene caller. "We can work that out."

"What about other kinds of distance?"

She asks what he means, knowing full well. "Distance can be bridged."

"Yes—even spiritual distance. Have you prayed like I suggested?"

Mind racing ahead, in microseconds her thoughts traversing universes of uncertainty, parsing the level of dishonesty to be employed, a flash of *how can we get through this and be a normal loving couple if I'm starting out with a lie*? And what exactly are you doing, Sissy, flirting with this long-ago and faraway boy from Edgewater County? A little church boy?

"I've been trying. Really, I have..."

"Well, now... how hard is it to pray?"

"...trying to open my heart, like you told me—you know in yoga, we'd call that opening the heart chakra—and then, I —I pray. But it's in my own way."

"And afterwards, how do you feel?"

"I feel good," a bald lie. "Warm inside."

True that: at the sound of his voice. Not knowing if anyone mystical's come into her heart besides Mitch, though.

"Keep on with that. You won't be sorry. Open yourself up to God's love."

Impatience, wanting to offer her own love. "Did you hear what I said in my message?"

"About coming up there to New York? Of course, that's why I called."

"No. At the end," in the same strangled voice as when saying the words in question.

"Oh... that was so sweet. Back at you, Lucy." A pause. "I'll think about coming to visit. Like I said... I'm kind-of busy these days."

"Think about it. Think about *me*," and letting the idea float like bait for a beat or two. A husky, sexy addendum: "Think about me *waiting* for you."

Awkward exit talk, no terms of endearment nor pledges of deep emotion offered. The Motorola flip phone warm against her ear, she holds it there even after Mitch's terse goodbye.

MONTHS PASSING. Mitch not on the social networking site as much, chatting less, a nonexistent response to a long, heartfelt email; Lucy, writing him another note, this one a degree more explicit in describing yearnings and feelings and pleasures awaiting him in the great city to the north. Lucy, feeling idiotic the instant after hitting *Send*.

Regretful. Scaring him off. For-sure.

As expected, no reply to the second, salacious message at all, either. Lucy, wasting time pursuing a man she'll never have, not unlike in high school. Lucy, realizing now the idea and memory of Mitch way different from the current version. Welcoming this dry and logically analytical voice.

But her feelings, persisting. Calling him to leave a long, rambling message, becoming crumbly halfway through, apologizing.

A day later, a card comes in the mail, with a South Carolina postmark! Mitch.

But it's a big fail: he took the time to hand-write a note telling her how sorry he was but that he thought their relationship, if not inappropriate, might simply be untenable for reasons practical and now, shockingly, otherwise:

> Lucy:
>
> To tell the truth, and we always should, I've met someone through my church. I'm sorry, but she feels as though sent to me, and I to her. I cannot wait for you to meet her one day. Kirsten and I seem to make a good team, like we're made for one another. Like the Lord brought us together.
>
> That said, I don't see why we can't continue to be close friends, just as we've always been. I'm writing this to you not to hurt you, but because I didn't want you to think anything else was possible. Not now that Kirsten's been sent to me like this. Life, and love, is a mystery to all of us but Him.
>
> Take care, Lucy. Please don't be upset. Keep me posted.
>
> Yours in Christ, M.

And the coup de grâce? She logged onto her social media account to find Mitch, and their entire message history, gone.

Rage. His fucking card counted for nothing—he'd ghosted her!

She screams and flings her computer keyboard across the room, a shower of plastic keys raining onto the floor after it strikes the corner of the desk where she keeps up with her business papers and data.

LUCY. Not thinking about him, thinking about him, either way finding herself drinking more than ever.

It's not Mitch per se, the thought finally strikes. *It's what he represents—her fading youth.*

Getting sloppy drunk one night with the younger crowd, throwing back shots. Porter, the musician she'd already dated once, comes home with her. Bumping into one another on the sidewalk, playful and laughing, then: kissing, deep, passionate, under a glowing orange streetlamp that made them both look embalmed.

"I've missed you."

"You, too."

Slurping. Groping. Grunting.

At home, proceeding to the matter at hand with enthusiasm. Lucy, bucking up against him, febrile and sustained, but so drunk she can't come. Wearing him out. Unconsciousness.

WAKING up in shafts of morning light, startled. Porter, snoozing, cute as can be.

Wait—Porter? Je-sus.

The evening flooded back to her, as does her broken

personal commitment regarding how there'd be no more of these meaningless, rutting nights of physical non-love. *Ugh.*

Cramping. Lucy, so sloshed last night she forgot the monthly visitor's arrival had been imminent. Lost in the moment, grateful to have a hot bod close to hers. Inside her. Forgetting her troubles. But, *forgetting*.

Reaching down and feeling dampness. Throwing back the covers. And next, an involuntary yelp of shock:

Bedsheets and legs soaked like finding the horse's head in *The Godfather*; a crime scene, she vaguely remembers Porter loving her with intense focus and a measured, powerful stroke, moaning with pleasure:

"Baby, my god—you are the wettest thing I've ever felt..."

Praying for a way out of this with dignity.

Groggy, turning over, smacking and clicking his dry, hungover lips and tongue, Porter says, "Hey, sweet thing... g'morning." Looking over at her. Then down at her body.

Throwing back his part of the damp sheet, his thighs covered in dried blood, penis flopping over stained crimson like a strawberry popsicle. "Whoa."

"Oh, honey—this is horrific."

"It's okay." Blinking his eyes, he swallows. Hard. "Really, wow, excuse me..."

Up and out of bed, he bolts across the bedroom, his tight bike-rider butt cute sporting a spatter of Lucy-blood on one cheek. Porter, slamming the bathroom door.

Retching and groaning: a death rattle. "*Hoof, hoof.*"

The sound of the toilet flushing, next the shower running.

Lucy, thinking about joining him, but not doing so. Porter, later, a friendly kiss, reassurances that it's all good, a story they'll tell in not-so polite company one day, and last, a sincere promise to call. "We'll hang out. It was—great."

"Super. Awesome."

As the echo of the slammed door faded into silence, she knows:

A turning point.

FEELING BUT AN INSECT among the thrumming asphalt and glass towers of the grand city, lost among her friends and associates, none of them family, Lucy, alone, feels the weight of her father's disapproval from beyond the grave, his disdain and apparent shame for her body, always telling her to change her clothes, to cover herself, to subsume her pulchritude, her sexuality. Lucy, unable to fully open up to people, to give herself to someone. To let them in.

Lucy, loving her father more than words adequate to express, but never feeling that love back. Never being able to satisfy him, a yearning, yawning chasm; never forgiving her for leaving South Carolina for New York—for anywhere. But reminding herself that now, never needing to seek his approbation again. The funeral months in the past, but a moment no less cathartic, a farewell, overdue but final. Forgiveness, to an extent. What did her father's disapproval matter now?

A sea-change: Lucy, moving back south, not caring about the heat and the humidity and the corn-pone good old boys, her inheritance and proceeds from the sale of the family home making possible an investment: A yoga studio in northeast Columbia, a good location on the outskirts of the Piedmont Tech campus and smack-dab amidst several high-dollar mega-mansion suburbs built in the time since she'd left. Lucy, running a few ads and acquiring an immediate and loyal following. An expert motivator; a long and lithe and living example. Toned. Owned. She gained clients, more than enough. Getting a condo, a townhouse, at the lake.

Seeing her homeland through fresh eyes. A beautiful place, really. Walking around the yard for the last time, looking at the house, the old family land, the curve on the road where she used to stand and dream of being swept up and taken away to another place, a different place... she didn't mind coming back home, in fact she prospered, but could never have lived here again.

One night at the marina restaurant on the lake, Lucy and Mitch, running into each other while she dined out with Timmy and his brood; Mitch, his fiancée in tow, a real cutie, seems nervous. Lucy, thinking, *no wonder he lost interest*: the fabled Kirsten a Kewpie doll ten years his junior, as shiny and beatific as Mitch himself seems.

"I'm shocked," Mitch says at the news she's returned to South Carolina. "I thought you said you'd never come back here."

"When I came down for my father's funeral, I guess I felt the tug. A big change came over me."

"Change—does that mean you took my advice?"

Lucy, turning and gesturing to her family gathered around the dinner table, breaking bread—the kids well behaved, Timmy cordial and relaxed, seeming to be happy to have his sister there with him in the land of their mutual birth. "Sure. I opened my heart. And this is what I found."

His fiancée, tittering and working her blonde eyebrows up and down. "You should come to our church. I mean, not only did I find *Him* there, but I found Mr. Right, too," squeezing herself to her man. "Maybe you could be so lucky."

Lucy, smiling and sipping a glass of Perrier with a slice of lime and smiling; the spirit, glowing and alight within her, a notion of assurance beyond feeling, the way she'd heard finding the Lord dwelling in one's heart described, certitude beyond normal, measurable emotion: "Oh, honey, I don't need to find the right person."

"No?"

"Nah. *He* needs to find *me*."

Besides, in addition to being busy at her trade, new creative projects loom. Not the painting; writing! She'd started a notebook of Edgewater County memories. The first vignette's about the death of her grandmother, which Lucy witnessed at seven. And lighter anecdotes, like a day when Uncle Junior took them out driving in his muscle car and got into trouble for it. They say to write what you know.

But beyond the short stories she's become the author of the story that is her everyday life; Lucy now turns the page in more ways than one. And it feels freaking great.

trauma and restoration

THE SOUND OF THE CRASH—HORRENDOUS, explosive, and nearby—wrenches me out of a vivid REM sleep cycle. I squawk like a shot goose and stagger, bed-blind and tangled up in sheets, into the hallway. My dreams, already fraught with metaphoric anxieties corresponding to an ongoing daytime conflict, had been troubled enough already.

Confusion at the inky dark, which shouldn't be, as there's a nightlight out here for Polly. Much becomes apparent—that *ker-blam* wasn't an attack on the homeland by terrorists, only the transformer across the street blowing out. Again. Damn rural electric co-op—next best thing to being off the grid.

My daughter's voice comes muffled by the closed door of her room. "Daddy?"

"It's okay, babygirl. The power's out. It's the transformer. That's all."

"No, it isn't."

"Sure it is."

"No—I hear voices. It's something else."

Now my wife Becca's voice, equally distant, from downstairs in the master. I've been sleeping up here in the guest room for a few months. Long story. "Timmy?"

"*Transformer across the street blew*," I call out. "*It's not a crisis.*"

We meet on the stairs, our flashlight beams mingling like those of Mulder and Scully on *The X-Files*, our all-time fav TV show.

"Blew from what?"

Shrugging. "Who knows...?"

Becca pulls a shimmery half-robe tight. She looks sexy as hell—oh, how we want what we currently cannot have. "That scared the living mud out of me."

"Me-too. Did I sleep through a storm?"

Shaking her head. "The thunder would've woken me."

Polly, shrieking from inside her room: "Mommy? *What's going on?*"

"I told her it was okay."

Becca moves me aside and says in her reassuring Mommy cadence, "It's okay, angel. The power's off, it's nothing... mom's coming."

My wife shines her light back in my face. "Tim—are you going to go outside and make sure everything's okay?"

"*Duh*. Go check on the babygirl."

Polly, ten and a beanpole like daddy used to be before turning into more of a piece of fruit (read: apple), has been skittish all her life, neurotic, a handful—I don't know where she gets it from, really I don't. Twitchy and prone to anxiety, but so smart, our little reader, fast as I can download books onto her iPad. Sensitive, though. Sensitive to this world. Sensitive to what's going on with her folks, this business about Daddy and Mommy sleeping at opposite ends of the house. Impossible to ignore for either of us, much less the kidlet.

Polly's confronted us about the situation at inopportune, surprising moments: During a sleepyhead Sunday brunch at a crowded Café Strudel, and at a Friday night home-cooked dinner with her one set of surviving grandparents: Becca's folks, who live in Lexington.

"Daddy doesn't love Mommy," our daughter said all matter-of-fact while digging into a piece of grandma's Mississippi Mudslide cake. "They don't sleep together anymore. Nope."

Gray expressions of shock and discomfort flitted across the lined and soft-fleshed faces of her parents; throat-clearing, the tinkling of flatware against plates, Becca's mother calling to the tattooed server shuffling around in her the black-on-black Chuck Taylors to bring forth another mimosa, all the while keeping two red narrow slits trained on me—she loves her daughter. Mistrusts me, now. Eh—it is what it is, like the dudes on the TV talk shows so often say.

Dad, on the other hand, sat through it all completely pokerfaced, sipping his decaf cappuccino and humming a song cheerful but tuneless.

"Anyway," Polly continued despite our glares, "I just don't know what to think."

Grandpa set down his cup. "That's not any of your business, young lady. Nor is it ours. Hush, now."

Becca, going pish-posh. "It's because of our mutual snoring. Polly knows that's why."

Thank you, my eyes said; hers, more like: *Next time, cover your own ass.*

AND THEN THIS, a day or two ago, when I'd picked her up from gymnastics, which the kidlet wants to quit.

The two of us, sitting in an idling line of hungry consumers who'd also decided to make a run for the border, as it were, when, in the midst of smalltalk, she blurted, "What does it mean that you and Mom aren't—"

"Ask your mother," I said.

"I did."

"And?"

"Snoring."

I stared straight ahead, gripping the wheel. The car in front crept forward while I sat immobile, trying to figure out what to say.

A stupendous blaring honk rattled the frame of our modest sedan, coming from the gigantic, looming grill of the F-350 to the rear of us. It's a helpful reminder that everyone in this drive-through—everyone, and I mean everyone, but most especially the driver of this vehicle—is in a righteous godawful hurry to get this food and be on their way.

"Relax already, ass-wipe," waving in the rearview. "Sheesh."

"Potty-mouth."

"Yeah, yeah."

"Anyway...?"

"Snoring is the official family reason, and for now I'm sticking with that."

"All right, then, let's accept this reason as fact," she said, arguing like a little barrister before the bar, "if we may. Is it caused by your asthma? This 'snoring'? Did you just start this recently? Or did she just finally get tired of it."

"Sheesh." I didn't want to lie. "I've always had asthma; I've always snored."

"But if you've always snored, then that can't be the reason." She pounded her thigh with a closed fist, troubled but pleased at having caught me in a plot hole. "*Hah.*"

I pulled up to the window, paid the smiling moonfaced girl, took the bag. I handed the bean burritos to my daughter, put the tub of iced tea in the cup holder and pulled over into a parking space facing the fish place on the next outlying concrete pad. The color scheme, a rich royal blue, contrasted nicely with the desert pastels of the taco joint.

"We're fine," I said, cradling the bag of warm fast food against my body.

"I don't believe you."

"I'm talking about our order—it's all here."

My own daughter scoffed at me. "Snoring, my eye."

Once home Polly stopped me at the front door, insisted on hugging. Tight. Holding on.

"Please," her brown eyes—my eyes—nailing me to the wall.

"Please what, cutie patootie?"

"I just love us so much. Our little family."

My personal sprinkler system threatened to cycle on.

I blurted in a cracked voice, "Daddy loves you, too. And Mommy. Very much."

Pushing back from me, staring upward. A statement of intent. "I love all of us. *Together*."

"We're together," I insisted, feeling kicked in the stomach. "Stop worrying."

As the garage door opens, but only after I've stepped into the dusty Crocs I wear when doing yard work, the first thing that hits me is the smell, sharp and unnatural, of antifreeze. And, gasoline. I flip on the driveway floodlights.

A dozen yards in front of me, at the end of my driveway

curving inward from the peaceful avenue, is a body—a human body.

Frozen in my tracks.

I shine my flashlight down the driveway: here lies a young girl, sprawled, supine, as though she's in a grassy field counting meteors.

The sight of my neighbor Carlton rushing heavy-footed into my tepid pool of light spurs me into action. I fall down on my knees beside the girl. Her eyes stare straight up, lips parted like they tell you to do before snapping your school portrait. A trickle of blood leaking out of one pierced ear is the sole detail indicating that something's terribly wrong.

The girl's face is paler than pale. "Carlton—is she—?"

"Hold the light on her." Carlton places two thick sausage-fingers on her neck. "Lord have mercy. She's gone."

I curse in disbelief. A dead girl, not much older than my own kid. "What on earth happened?"

An enormous, gregarious man retired from a state highway department desk job, Carlton's tone is uncharacteristically brusque and unemotional, like that of a cop: "Vehicle versus transformer, the one in my yard. Two ejected, one still in the car."

All the utility lines here are buried underground, so on every block or so there's a boxy green transformer in the corner of someone's yard, including Carlton's. It appears I was only half wrong about the explosion and subsequent lack of power.

"They must-a come flying around the curve... I don't even *see* the transformer casing. Got something we can cover her up with?"

A tarp, I say with a shaking voice. "In the garage."

"Meet me in the street." Carlton, sporting an enormous black T-shirt and size 48 boxers with an all-over print of little red Tabasco bottles, runs out of my flashlight beam. For a man of such size, he appears light on his substantial, flip-flopping slabs of feet.

In the garage, a feeling of shock settles—I've never seen a dead person except in the context of tearful loved ones wearing Sunday clothes. And this, a dead child. Dizzy and panicked, I fumble to grab a tarp from the pile of camping gear stashed on a high shelf in the cluttered garage.

On the way back outside flashlight finds the staring faces of Becca and Polly in the doorway leading from the mud room into the garage.

"Daddy, what's wrong?"

"Get back," I say, stern. Then, quieter and calmer: "Just stay inside, ladies. There's been a car accident."

Polly, titillated: "Oh—I want to see!"

I make hard eye contact with my wife. "*No,*" I say, cutting and vicious. "Forget it."

"Come on, sweetie. Let's let Daddy go look first."

I bundle the tarp under my arm and head back outside. "*Do not come out here.* Is that understood?"

"Yes, *sir,*" Polly says, snide and pouty. "Mommy, please let me."

"Daddy says no, honey."

As I drape it over the body, the tarp crackles in a sad way that makes my stomach roll. The act seems more disrespectful than appropriate, if not premature—light reflects off her brown eyes, making it seem as though they moved to follow my approach. This human being is still so close to having been alive that she doesn't yet look dead. Not quite. But she is.

SEVERAL MONTHS AGO, on a long lunch break from teaching my one class at my alma mater, I drove around in the Cherokee listening to music on WSEU, the campus station. I needed a mental health break. My sister Lucy had called to say she'd written a book of short stories about our childhood, wanting me to read the manuscript. The kind of thing I'd once dreamed of doing.

Okay, then. Now Lucy's a writer. It's fine.

Remembering the college days and the first couple of years after, when we'd still rented not far from campus and lived in the city, my ad writing years... my goodness. How those had seemed like the golden days.

Next: We got married, moving out of the mill village with its crime and boho atmosphere to settle, for a time, into an upscale apartment complex. Gated and safe, soon after—sooner than we'd planned—Polly had come along, our little miracle surprise baby.

Family equaled house. Not an apartment. Instead of writing a great novel one day, the overarching question of existence had become: How much home could we buy on the modest resources, and credit score, we had?

Not much, as it happened—not in town, anyway, and not what I was making as a copywriter for a minuscule agency, a job that felt like manufacturing dog kibble. We didn't and don't have a dog, then or now, and as far as settling down I'd never much thought about having a yard with a fence and the upkeep and the responsibility of ownership; as far as I was concerned, we could rent from now until doomsday.

But that was before the kid; and before I put the idea of grad school on hold; and before I got locked into the job I still have, at a bigger agency and as a well-paid ad guy. Through promotion and effort, I've moved up the dog-food chain.

Even before the kid, though, Daddy had already been on

my ass about buying instead of renting. My office wasn't downtown, as he pointed out; I already had to drive halfway around the beltway every morning. So, as he reasoned, we ought to look out in the rural counties, where I could find bedroom communities and small, well-funded school districts, lower crime rates, and more bang for the buck house-wise. Like, *say*, back home in Edgewater County. And that, if I did choose this path, I could count on his financial help.

Only, as I thought to myself, if it's closer to the lake country than the scrubby backwoods halfway between Tillman Falls and Red Mound, where my sister and I grew up. I didn't want to live that far out. Maybe one day, in the family house my sister and I would one day inherit. But not anytime soon.

"Get in over your head with some overvalued old bungalow in Herndon Hill? No, sir. You ain't never getting the money back out of them things over yonder in Columbia. Not at these interest rates." A country boy, but a wise one. "But, a sound investment in a good brick house with low property taxes and room for that little baby to run and play? Now that I'd like to help you do. For your girls." On his advice we looked, and bought, above the lake in a placid, established neighborhood of contemporaries built in the 70s, just on the other side of the county line, indeed saving us quite a bit in property taxes, as well as on the price of the house itself. So much house for the money, at least compared to what we'd been shown in-town! It's a retro-hip split-level we've updated and added a screened porch onto and all sorts of landscaping touches, like the row of red tips which give us privacy from the houses across the way, like Carlton's. Ten years in the dump. Twelve, now, since we married. And fifteen since we started dating as Southeastern University seniors.

Wait—fifteen years since college? Forty, looming and inexorable, on the horizon?

Is it time for this midlife crisis bullshit?

Already?

That day I drove around listening to college rock and reminiscing. I got a milkshake and parked down in the Old Market, the college ghetto next to campus. Watched them all, the young, going about their carefree business. Nothing on the surface had changed, except for me with my fat old married Daddy self. Felt like Billy Pilgrim. I'd blinked my eyes and arrived at this moment! And yet I was still that guy I saw going into the coffee shop with his book bag. Or even younger—still the frightened adolescent riding around on dirt roads in the back seat of his uncle's muscle car.

Still this. Still that. None of it me.

Walked in from work later that day, a Tuesday, and told Becca I felt 'this' wasn't working; that after ten years I spend half my life driving back and forth from Edgewater County, that if she didn't want to move back into town, I wanted a separation. A place of my own. Close-in, as the realtors say.

All had been a mistake, in other words. Every bit of it.

Ton of bricks to hear her tell it, but I thought, and said, that the vibe I got from her had been equivalent to mine—one of ennui and disengagement. She looked at me like I was nuts. Said, *For heaven's sake, Tim.*

She asked who it was. How long it'd been going on.

I said, no one. Which was and is the truth.

At first Becca didn't believe me, but when I insisted it wasn't that kind of crisis, she acted relieved. Said, we can separate, but asked that I didn't actually leave-leave.

"For Polly's sake," Becca explained, crying, "just move upstairs. But don't move out. I'm a big girl—I don't need you. But she does."

"That's what I'm trying to say." This, the problem, though one I manufactured on the spot, repeating dialogue from some rom-com movie or TV show, probably. "You—you don't need taking care of. I need to be needed, and not just by Polly. By you, too. I—I don't know what your needs are. Or how to fulfill them."

She called me names, told me I needed therapy. Said she couldn't do any more to please anyone in the house than she was already doing. I moved into the guest room, but otherwise in our filial relations we've gone on like normal. Around Polly, at least.

My chest tight with anxiety, I bolt around the row of red tips and into the street. On the other side of the hedge is a steaming wreck of a car, a boxy sedan in a color that, in the ochre glow of the street lamps—on a different circuit, I guess?—registers as a neutral shade impossible to pin down.

On Carlton's sloping lawn, a second child's body is stretched out.

"Over here, Tim. Another head injury."

On closer inspection, the girl's alive, but convulsing.

Breathless, my heart flutters like the time in college I smoked pot with a guy I didn't know who forget to tell me the dope was from Hawaii and had been specifically bred to have an intense, climbing, mind-blowing high, and I began having palpitations and thought I was on the verge of a heart attack.

Calm down, a stentorian voice says. *You are the Daddy.*

"This beats all I've ever seen," I manage to say. "Mercy."

A wail issues from the wreck, a steaming lump of metal sitting sideways in the street.

"Go and talk to the other girl," Carlton whispers. "We can't do nothing for this one till the EMTs get here."

I sprint over in my dirty green Crocs and peer into the vehicle: All the glass is shattered, the engine block shoved halfway into the front seat, a reek of oil and gas leaking onto the perfect asphalt of Tea Olive Way—the streets were resurfaced this spring, and ever since skateboarders and roller-blade enthusiasts have been in absolute hog heaven. And now, this.

At first I can't discern the girl, but as I go around to the side I can see in a shaft of orange streetlight the flesh of a pale forearm, hanging at an angle.

"Oh, please help me," a tiny voice gurgles. "Please get me out."

Ice in my veins. I sweep the flashlight around inside the wreckage.

Yet another teen girl, but this one turns out to be the biggest gut punch of them all. In a rush of fresh horror, I realize I know her:

Alana Gormick lives three streets over and often sits for Polly, the latest time not three weeks ago, when Becca and I went out for a rare midweek dinner to have private time and talk out the difficulties we've been suffering. More accurately: difficulties I've been suffering, these gnawing questions about who I am and why I'm here, the kind of bullshit, I've now realized, that disappears once you look into the eyes of your worried kid. Or at least ought to disappear, like vapor from wintertime breath.

"Alana...?" I ask if she's all right. I try to keep my voice steady.

"Mr. Latham, is that you...?" A friendly, familiar face seems to have terrified her anew: "*Oh god please get me out of here please please please!*"

The Daddy voice reminds me to project calm and control.

"Now, you just relax, sweetie—help's on the way. You're going to be all right."

Her body's twisted at an odd angle, the other arm behind her; with her shaking, free hand, she reaches for me. For help.

Alana blinks rivulets of blood out of her eyes. "Please."

Helplessness, a sick wave through me. I start yanking at the rear door on the driver's side, but it's wedged tight. "You just hang in there, honey… the firemen and police and ambulance are almost here."

"*Don't leave me.*"

"I wouldn't do that in a million years. Not for all the beans in Boston would I leave a pretty girl like you behind." I try to laugh. She smiles back, weeps anew.

The first deep, violet flashing appears from around the corner, and a highway patrol unit pulls up behind the leaking heap of the car.

"Well, it's about goddamn time," I blurt, an involuntary release of my fear. *"We need help over here!"*

The patrolman trots over, directing his cop flashlight at me and into the car at Alana. To me, he looks not much older than the girls—a rookie, stuck working a quiet night shift out in the sticks.

The patrolman speaks into his shoulder mic, various codes and instructions. "What do we have here, sir?"

"*Help me*," Alana screams. "Help us."

"Hold on, ma'am." All matter of fact. Sees it every day, probably.

Probably? Of course he does. "Vehicle versus electrical transformer."

Trauma and Restoration 197

WITHIN THE NEXT five minutes activity around the crash site increases at an exponential degree: More cops, the EMTs, other neighbors appearing on lawns.

After I show the dead girl on the driveway to the rescue guys, I run into the house to check on my own ladies.

Becca meets me in the kitchen, our flashlights again commingling. "Tim—?"

"They hit the transformer. Three little girls."

"Little girls—?"

"Teens," in clarification. "One's the sitter. Alana Gormick."

"Oh, god—" Becca covers her mouth. "Is she dead?"

"Not Alana. But the one on our driveway is."

My wife screams.

And now Polly, who's been listening from the pitch-dark of the living room, joins in. "What's wrong with Alana? *What's wrong with ALANA?*"

"Call Alana's folks," I order like the captain on deck. "And say there's been an accident. That—that they should hurry over here." I bolt back outside without waiting for a response.

A MORE SENIOR highway patrol officer arrives on the scene, asking to speak with me—one of the witnesses, such as I am.

"Did you observe the incident, sir?"

"No, I was dead asleep," regretting my choice of words. "I heard it, sort of."

"We're going to be in and out of your driveway for a bit," he tells me. "Have your family to stay inside, if you don't mind, till we get this scene processed."

"This is terrible."

His face, stony, and voice quite flat. "Yes sir, it surely is."

As the creeping dawn approaches, the noise level outside turns downright cacophonous, the activity made more surreal by the early hour—normally a time of peaceful birdsong and placid, pink light, here like an outtake from APOCALYPSE NOW, only the medivac helicopter's not flying over in slow motion.

All through the process of cutting her out of the wreckage, Alana has continued to scream out my name. I try to comfort her, but I'm told to stand to the side, please.

LATER, in the full sun of morning, a reporter from the local CBS affiliate shoves a microphone in my face and asks me a few questions—boilerplate interrogatives, *tell us what happened*, that type-deal.

"I came out in my robe and slippers, and there she was."

The reporter, her shiny eyes imploring me for elaboration, nods and smiles. "I see. And—?"

"And that was that."

I show them a spot of dried blood. The shooter walks over with the mini-cam and points the lens downward.

I wave him off. "Stop—I don't want that girl's parents seeing that on TV."

The camera guy, young and pierced in various places, pulls the lens away with a sigh. "It's just B-roll, dude."

The reporter further assures me they won't use the shot. "Anything else you want to say?"

I don't want to seem flippant, or offer flowery platitudes merely for the sake of doing so, but it's all I have: "It's just a hell of a thing. A real—tragedy."

After the news crew leaves I splatter bleach onto the

driveway blood, which is maybe the size of a grapefruit or a softball. I let the bleach sit while I go get a wire brush.

I'M WATCHING the power company finishing up their work in Carlton's yard. The old transformer casing had been thrown over a hundred feet; one cop said he thought they took the curve doing over seventy.

A sheriff's deputy, as it turns out, had passed the girls a few miles back toward town, but remembers seeing nothing out of the ordinary. The emerging theory? Out joyriding without a license in a sleeping grandmother's car, the girls must have been spooked by that same passing deputy. Hauling ass home. For the last time...

An SUV pulls up, and I see that it's Alana's father slipping tiredly out of the driver's side. Pete Gormick looks grim, his skin papery and splotchy, like a dying old man. He's neither old nor dying, of course—but for all I know, his daughter might be.

He trudges up the driveway, offers a limp wave. "Tim."

"How is she?"

"Not good. She—the surgery on her arm, it went fine, but..." He bursts into tears. "I couldn't sit still and wait for my own baby girl to come out of recovery. Jesus..."

I hold out my arms and this man I barely know collapses against me. I help him regain himself, which he does, nodding and self-conscious.

"It's just a hell of a thing," I say. More weak-sauce platitudes. "Hang tough."

Pete calms down. Perhaps my ineffectual bromides, offering as they do a kind of acknowledgment but only in a vague and innocuous manner, are the right things to say after all.

He nods and gropes for words. Surveying my neat yard, his eyes land nowhere near my own gaze. "I just had to come and see where it happened. Not that I haven't been down this street, and around that curve, a thousand times... you know?"

"I was dead asleep," my poor-taste phrasing again. "Thought a bomb went off."

He laughs, bitter. "Might as well have been. Like one of those, those *people* overseas in the Middle East. Kids. Victims. Bombings. You know?"

I didn't think it was the same, but I told him I got it.

"They think she'll be fine. That's the main thing. She was lucky," he says, making brief eye contact. "That's how she's doing, by the way. I'm rambling. I could use a drink. Or maybe not. She's going to be okay, though. Right?"

"I'm no doctor, but all things considered, I'd say so. She's alive. Yeah?"

"What did she say to you? She was awake in the car, or so they tell me."

My blood runs cold. "She—she begged me to help her."

"Oh."

"But I couldn't." My eyes begin watering. "Couldn't—couldn't get the door open."

Gormick clasps my hand, strong, and claps me on the shoulder. "What, you're Superman? Forget about it."

"I tried."

"Christ," he says, dismissive. "Forget it."

I said I would try.

Pete's opportunity to be strong for me, now, seems to have fortified his spirits. He slaps his hands together as though ready to tackle a home improvement project. "Well—I've got to get back on over there. To my family."

"Let us know how she is. Polly's losing her mind to come to the hospital, but..."

"No, no. The waiting room's overflowing as it is."

Like a shot he's back into his Escalade, tires squealing on the smooth pavement until disappearing around the deadly corner.

I SHOWER, try to nap, unsuccessful. At six, we gather as a family to watch the news.

"It's a hell of a thing," I say on TV, my voice sounding reedy and more Southern than I expected to hear. Worse, in the horrid close up that little tattooed twerp of a cameraman took, I appear pink, overfed, swollen. They don't use the blood shot, at least.

Becca turns it off. "Enough of this. Enough for one day."

We decide to grill hamburgers for dinner, something fun to take Polly's mind off the accident.

While I drink a cold beer on the patio and wait for the coals to cook down, I watch through the kitchen window as Becca preps the burger-fixings. She's a glorious woman, my wife. There, in front of me. Alive and beautiful and with that little flush she gets in her cheeks, a splotch of blood that's the good kind, coursing inside healthy and living veins.

She comes outside. Becca wonders why the dead girl and her friends, more than a year away from getting driver's licenses, would take a car out to go joyriding. She wonders where the parents were, for three young girls to get their hands on a car and go tearing around Edgewater County in the middle of the night.

"Maybe their folks were caught up in their own shit. Didn't notice."

"They grow up fast nowadays. Not like us."

"Our girl's not going to run wild like that," I declaim with certitude, challenging and daring a universe of possibility over which I have no control. "Not Polly."

"You hope she won't. There's only so much a parent can do."

"I know—but she's got a good family here. Strong." I reach across and touch my wife's hand, the first gesture of affection I've made toward her in some time. "A loving family."

She squeezes back. "You must be exhausted."

"I am." My voice cracks, but no more tears. "Big time."

"Thanks for making me stay inside, by the way."

"No need for us both to carry around those pictures in our heads."

"Let's try to make you forget them, too," she says, kissing me.

"That mean I'm coming back to the bed?"

"You're the one who left it. Over it all, are you?"

My face heats up like the charcoal in the grill. "I don't think there's anything to be over. Never was, I mean."

I reach over and pull my wife close. Her body offers me comfort and warmth. She is whole and alive, as is Polly.

As am I.

My stomach rumbles. "Let's get the sizzle on."

"Light the mosquito torches, too. We'll come sit with you while the burgers cook."

The air out on the patio is filled with charcoal and smoke, but I breathe deeply anyway. I can still taste the acrid smell of the wreck—of death—at the back of my teeth, and I want to get rid of the sensation.

Our dinner, those ordinary charcoal-grilled burgers, oven baked fries, and ice cream sandwiches, seems the best I've tasted in my entire life. We discuss the Sunday that's ahead of us, and come to a group decision: to fritter away the afternoon at a park. To picnic, stretch out on the grass, read books, play, laugh. Nowhere to get to, nowhere to be. Later, as its gets dark, we'll come home, my wife and babygirl and me. Together. For keeps. Sound like a plan?

button, her sister, their father, and lucky latham

An Excerpt From

Buddy Sykes brought home a troubled relationship with the war. His pal Tim 'Lucky' Latham from over near Red Mound made it home too, but left their friend Ronnie Pettus over there, which seemed to have affected them both in a manner acute.

Once, when Button and Thim, already a snooty little asshole, had been prepubescent schoolgirls, their father picked them up one afternoon and taken them for a side trip. It had surprised Button to see Mr. Latham, who worked at the IGA as the produce manager, sitting in the front seat of the car, a boxy Buick.

"We got to run ourselves a quick errand, me and Lucky." Her father, crinkling the ruddy skin around his blue eyes, both traits which he'd given her, but coupled with her Asian features always made for a striking combination that hadn't often been called beautiful or even pretty.

"*Where*," Thim demanded. "For what?"

"We need to run on over by the cemetery, and while we do, I want y'all to sit right here in the car and get started on your homework."

"Dad-da," Thim screeched, her face pinched. "But I don't want to."

"I don't wanna, neither." Button, echoing her big sister, because back then, Thim could do no wrong in her eyes. "Nuh-uh. Go home."

"Too bad, little angels." Her daddy, driving on over and turning into Forest Knoll Garden cemetery, scene of the action for ghosts and more ghosts, it seemed. "We'll get you home to Mom-mom soon enough."

"We old codgers won't be gone over yonder too long," Mr. Latham said in his country drawl, the thickest Edgewater County had to offer. "It's something we got to do, though. Your daddy and me."

"Yes sir," Button's daddy added with a solemn sigh. "Yes sir, it is." He clapped Lucky on the bony, middle-aged shoulder, both seeming froggy in their throats and wet-eyed in a way that Button never remembered seeing her father look.

Button and Thim both sat in silence and watched, but only Thim had been able to spy what was going on—Button, too short to see over the brick wall running along Common Street.

"They have their arms around each other!" Thim whispered. "And Mr. Lucky, he looks like he's crying."

"I want to go home," Button remembered saying. "I'm scared."

"Well, I'm not. But this is weird. Oh, my—I think Daddy is crying, too. Aw."

Button, going *boohoo*.

"Something's wrong. Something's really wrong." Thim gripped Button's tiny arm and snarled, the older sister's principal method of communication to her diminutive sibling. "I'm going to sort this out."

Button, remembering how Thim had blown the horn,

and the men raced back with red faces, annoyed but not yelling at them. A silent drive home, first dropping Lucky Latham off at the IGA where he worked.

Later, when she'd been older, Button asked her father about that particular day. He explained it had been the anniversary of Ronnie Ed Pettus dying over in Vietnam, how he and Lucky always paid tribute in the cemetery. It'd also been the first time she remembered seeing The Dixiana sign, and the mural on the side of the building, noticing because both men seemed to give the rooster a little wave as they passed. She assumed her father's reticence about discussing Vietnam and the war had to do with Ronnie Ed. Only later was she told that the reasons were more about national security issues than sentiment. That, and personal shame. A complicated story.

She'd always and forevermore associated The Dixiana with that first instance of consideration regarding death and loss, and the implications of being alive and then not, so maybe getting fired from the honkytonk, as she expected Rabbit would do today, had been in the cards all along: being stuck here in Tillman Falls felt like death for some time now, even before she'd left the first time, as a teenager going off to college.

Perhaps leaving The Dixiana would be like a resurrection. If only she didn't have her mother, and Grandpa Burnie, Button, at her still-young age, could decide how she wanted to live the rest of her life.

Hell, maybe she'd go out on tour again—that'd been the peak of her music-loving life, not working at the ramshackle old Dixiana, and not being the caretaker to the sick and the old and the dying. Phish tour—the first access to higher consciousness and sensing the high vibration of life as well as the nadir, dwelling deep down in puddles of muck. The thick strawberry goo of oblivion. A long time ago, now. Could one go home again?

the fable of samson & trudy
An Excerpt From

ON THE WAY HOME FROM GETTING REAMED OUT AND fired by Roy Earl Pettus, that son of a biscuit eater who, before he'd opened his smart mouth, she'd wanted to screw again—screw long and hard like back when they'd been kids—Trudy instead cussed him with such grief that she about run off the river highway and wrecked her Taurus, right as she passed by the bar that represented the other pole of her existence, Ape Hangers, though she still thought of it as Fast Traxx. The biker bar. Where her husband had lived half his life. What a topper on the day wrecking the car would've been.

Maybe it wouldn't have been an accident. The way Trudy had been feeling.

Through misty vision she whipped into the dirt of the driveway in the woods to the house, that durn old rotting hellhole she lived in back here with Mickey Samuelson. She ain't had crap, Trudy. Not before, and not now.

Except for the honkytonk.

And what does that little stuck-up shit Roy Earl do? His

granddaddy dies and then the little prince shows up waving a will, and takes it all away.

Took her job from her like it wasn't nothing.

Like she didn't mean nothing to him. That just couldn't be. Had to be some meaning in there. After what they had had together.

Thirty years ago.

Wasn't nothing but kids back then. She was the one giving it meaning. Not him. Not with his money and pretty wife down on that island.

Trudy, about as full of horseshit as they came.

Worse, as she sat stubbing out her cigarette in the filthy ashtray and checking her eyes to see how red they looked, Trudy couldn't say nothing to Samson about that old-lovers part of all this drama. About losing this job, and the history with Roy Earl that ought to've made a difference. All that she had to keep inside.

YEAH, she still thought of her husband by that nickname, as did everyone from what he called the old crew of proud, marauding Pagan Knights of Edgewater County. Trudy'd come along in his life long after those days of wild-ass riding on them choppers. Samson—Mickey—fifteen years older than her. A god-durn old man now, on social security.

And here only in her early 50s. Nowhere near the way he acted.

Maybe horny as hell. That much she felt. But not old.

At their height in the early '70s, brothers of the Pagan Knights biker club owned the two-lane blacktops all over the South Carolina midlands, but especially in Edgewater County.

Tension came from encounters at rallies with members of Trinity, based in Camden and rivals by dint of proximity, and the Scarabs, out of North Carolina and threatened less by geography than the size of the PK tribe. Mickey had big scrapbooks full of all sorts of pictures of the custom bikes he worked on with his brother Rusty, an airbrush virtuoso who painted and finished teardrop tanks while his older brother handled the engines and the mechanics. The two of them customized them motherfucking hogs better than anyone in Edgewater County, or Richland or Lexington Counties either, for that matter.

To her eyes and ears, these days Mickey spent too much time still thinking about himself as Samson the Pagan Knight. Weepy and regretful. Full of confessions about all manner of shit he pulled back in the day. And allusions to much worse, which creeped her out. Like beating people to death type stuff.

Facing it: Her hubby had turned into a creep in so many ways.

When he wasn't piss-drunk and crying, it was piss-angry, and sitting there smelling bad and with a black cloud all around him, an aura that Trudy swore she could half-see, not to sound like some hippy idiot like Button Sykes. In his decrepitude, as Trudy thought of her husband's decline, he had become a nasty and unpleasant human being. He always said he had been afraid of getting to where he couldn't ride, and with his lower back that had happened; afterwards, about 1990 or so, this one time when he come into her beloved honkytonk, The Dixiana, he had finally scooped her up and carried her off to his house back in the woods—right here— and done her hard and long with that big pecker of his, and later that year made her his wife: the redneck trailer park biker trophy wife. That's what Trudy Pirkle had been to Mickey Samuelson.

"I always liked you Pirkle girls, with your blue eyes and them long old bodies," he told her on their wedding night in Myrtle Beach, in a fancy fresh and modern condo set way up high and right there on the beach, and looking down she could almost jump out into that green deep Atlantic Ocean, all of which had made Trudy feel not like jumping but flying, like a character in a magical place, and how he had made love to her so tender that wedding night. Married.

"I feel like I done hit the jackpot." He whispered in her right hear as he lay breathing and damp in the aftermath of their explosive union, like nobody and nothing she'd ever had or felt. "My precious angel. "

"Stay in there. Stay hard in me, Samson."

And he had, moving on through another orgasm for both. They'd gotten drunk and partied with some crank and whippits and had sucked and fucked until both of them sore; she didn't half remember the rest of the night and the weekend. A blur of beer and shots and smoking and loving and fucking, afterwards him laid out snoring like a gut-stuck hog.

What she complaining about? She still had all that shit. Well—not the loving and fucking part. But that wasn't supposed to stay anyway.

Was it?

Samson, the old biker full of tales about riding up to North Carolina and communing with other clubs, the Brothers and the Outlaws and the Angels, and raising hell and getting drunk and riding them hogs around them mountain roads like it wasn't nothing to be shitfaced and hauling ass and laughing your way round those curves, and not a brother never ever had a wreck 'cause bikers were different, and lord but Trudy knew that wasn't nothing but looking back with rose-colored lenses. Rusty had told her how many bad drugs there were, how many fights, the wrecks people had. Legs on the asphalt one time, when this dude hit a concrete median and sent his girl flying across in front of a bus full of old people going to ride the Tweetsie Railroad. Legs on the road, he said, laughing.

"Yeah, it was all fun and games, them days," as Rusty said, smoking and sitting in his truck. This was back around 2000 when they was doing it, which was awful and wonderful and awful and what did anyone want from her? Let anyone judging her walk a mile in her boots. Like she heard someone say in a movie, a husband who was caught by his wife, 'it just happened.'

His brother had been the one to say, damn, we got to quit this mess. I feel guilty. And then she had, too. Awful, like she wanted to jump off the balcony at her tall Myrtle Beach honeymoon hotel. Or get throwed off the back of Samson's hog, have her legs split open on the road rather than laying sprawled in her brother-in-law's bed, him pumping away at her with a high, whining sound from deep inside his nose like a little kid worried about being caught doing something wrong. Which it was.

Karma. Like she had feared back when she fucked her boss's grandson.

Samson couldn't ride no more even if his fat ass wanted to —he couldn't hardly get out of his chair no more, but when he did, he still stood half a head taller than her. Could still half kill her, if he wanted to.

He hadn't hit her in ten years now, not since the time she said, "If it happens again, I'm-a gonna leave your fat ass back in here," and he had cried, cried like a baby—it wasn't like he didn't do that anyhow when he was that drunk. Cried like poor little Roy Earl had when she said no, angel. We can't do it no more. Mr. Rabbit—your Pa-Paw, as you call him—he's gonna cut our asses. He's gonna fire me.

And now, after thirty years, Roy Earl had gone and finally made it come true.

She felt like she was losing her mind. Now who couldn't stop crying, and who cracked open one of Mickey's tallboys, which made him holler out was that beer for him he had heard her opening up?

Why put it off?

She took a slug, belched. Went in to tell her husband what happened.

SHE SHOULDN'T NEVER HAD SAID nothing. Oh, mercy. Lord, at the hollering and cussing.

"Mickey, calm down. You gonna have a thrombo."

"I'm-a gonna go shove his goddamn head down one of them shit toilets in that goddurn firetrap piece of shit honky-tonk. Not worth a shit son of a bitch motherscratching Reynolds Pettus son of a whore. I'm gonna go and get my gun, Trudy. I'm gonna go and son of a bitch get my daddy's shotgun, oil that motherscratching son of a bitch and take it over and put a goddurn hole in that buttermilk-sucking, fat little faggot-ass bitch. Show him he can't walk in there and fire you, not after all you done for them bastards—"

He twisted around like he meant for real to go and get a gun, but regretted it. Yelling at the pain, cursing his swollen foot. Trudy could only watch in horror as Samson hobbled down the cramped hallway of the old house, which had been his daddy's house, a ramshackle construction with additions built on it every which way and set back in the woods off Highway 231. Every room and nook and cranny stacked with junk that'd accumulated across several generations of Samuelson men and their hobbies.

Hollering at his hurt foot. Yelling about Roy Earl.

Why not let him go and kill Roy Earl? That a-hole done ruined my life.

Roy Earl ruined her life, hadn't he. By not coming back for her after he got rich.

Shit. She was the one who had said "no" to him. But then, he'd been sixteen and her twenty-one at the time. These days they'd put you in jail for that.

But all she said: "You ain't going nowhere. Not with that foot of your'n."

ABOUT THAT LIFE OF HERS, living stuck out in these haunted redneck woods, where old people said all manner of mess had gone on back in colonial times—witchcraft, weirdness, wickedness like Coy Wando and the Tragedy of '77: like a specter of his former bad-ass self, Mickey sat in his own funk drinking three, three and a half cases a week of tallboys, smoked a carton of expensive-ass Marlboros and wanted hamburgers and fried steak or chicken every night, wouldn't budge on none of it. Ate and shit so much there wasn't no way she could keep up, hardly. Worked so much, six nights a week, still, but nonetheless expected to cook and clean house, and damn if she didn't care what happened from here.

Maybe Roy Earl and Mickey would kill each other, for all she knew.

Maybe they'd all get ebola and shit themselves bloody.

Maybe that son of a gun President Obola would make the world blow up. Michael Savage said on the radio every day that the boy-king wasn't worth a toot. Couldn't be trusted. That Pooty-Poot in Russia was laughing at us all.

Lord—when was this country gonna get a durn president

to believe in again? She swore the more she thought about it, not even Reagan. Not since JFK.

She fell across her stinky bed, the one in the small room where she slept because Mickey took up the whole queen bed, fairly hung over the side of it, not to mention his heinous sleep apnea, so bad she went online and googled Severe Snoring, and after that knew he would likely one day wake up dead, and he'd be free.

Or rather: she'd be free.

Which made her feel guilty to beat the band.

After a while she got him back in his chair, and got five or six beers in him and turned the DVR to last Sunday's NASCAR race, which he had not seen because he had gotten up that day and started in on a bottle of Jack Daniels and passed out by lunchtime. And she had been glad. Had had the rest of the day to herself.

She sat on the couch across from him. A flea jumped on her leg. She caught it, pinched it to death between her long, chipped fingernails she had been planning to work on at the bar the afternoon her sweet Mr. Rabbit passed away. "Don't do nothing, honey. We gonna be all right. Roy Earl don't know what he's saying. He's tore up over Rabbit. Over his granddaddy dying."

"I'm gonna whup his ass anyway."

"You ain't doing it tonight. Let's drink some beer together. Party, and look at the race. C'mon, sugar."

"Still gonna beat his ass," he'd say every now and then. Belching. Killing only his tallboys rather than rich Roy Earl.

She didn't want nothing bad to happen to Roy Earl. After screwing him back when he was a kid when she was a dumbass who ought to've known better, which she only done because she was drunk, she'd made the crucial mistake of feeling a spark there with that young'un. A baby-face, one she was just trying to show how he could go and make some other girl happy. Bad judgement all around.

But damn if she didn't get butterflies at thinking about doing it with him again. He seemed so smart, Rabbit's grandson. A pissant all full of himself. But successful and confident and handsome as hell. Look at what he had gone and done. Burnie Sykes said Roy Earl had sold his company, the chain of smoothie stands, for a million dollars.

Trudy, admitting to herself that she had stood there in that damn Dixiana dump for the last thirty-two years, and she'd be shit if not two or three times a week, like clockwork, she'd remember the night she kissed Roy Earl, and screwed him and screwed him some more, coming with him hard, and loving him and his deep brown eyes, and she would be goddurned if she didn't catch herself drifting, fantasizing, looking at Burnie's bald head nodding over his half-full mug. Saying to herself, what-if, what-if.

Maybe by now she and Roy would own The Dixiana together. Maybe Rabbit would've retired, and still be alive instead of keeling over in the street.

Damn that Roy Earl. Why had he never come back and gotten her.

As the years went on she had grown so bitter and rueful, particularly when Rabbit would come in shaking his head and saying, that boy done opened another one of them Spotted Banana™ Fruitshake joints of his, "This time down in Savannah," or wherever. "He's gonna make him a mint. Boy, I musta done something right."

"You must've."

Faraway, usually. And rueful, too: "My grandbaby's a good boy. Yes, he is."

Come back and get me, Roy Earl, as she had thought so often. Had sent it out there to him. She knew it was stupid.

Couldn't remember the last time she had prayed for him to come and get her. Probably after he got married, finally, to that stuck-up Rucker bitch. Her brother Devin had been so cute, too. She never knew what happened to him. A drunk, if memory served.

MICKEY—THE mighty Samson—lay grinding his teeth and snoring in his chair, and so she put on *The Walking Dead* instead of the end of the race. Mickey, letting one of them awful old beer farts there in his sleep. He didn't know he was doing it, bless his heart. She lit a scented candle she had bought over at the hippie shop in Columbia, patchouli rose.

His bad toenail was what she had to worry about, a thick one that had started running with pus. She would unwrap in the morning and look again and rinse it off again with peroxide. He liked to couldn't walk on it no more, but mercy, with his bad knees Samson couldn't but hardly walk as it was—they sounded like popcorn popping when he would stoop or try to squat or sit—and with his ankles always swelling up, too. She had to get that weight off him. She couldn't do it with a bad toe and bad knees, but she had to start walking him.

Trudy, she hadn't never had an ounce of fat on her. Too skinny. Men liked some meat on the bones. Not too much. More than a Pirkle girl from over in Red Mound had. Mickey Samuelson had loved her bony butt, though. Didn't he.

TRUDY, leaving him in his chair to go to look through her old high school annuals, at the signatures of boyfriends and guys who'd had crushes on her lanky, longlegged Pirkle ass. She didn't cry or anything dramatic like that. You didn't cry over all that mess, not that long ago, not in your 50s. That's what she'd learned. She wished she had realized about growing old back when she shacked up with Samson, so much older than her and married once before and with a kid by that one and another'n that had showed up one Thanksgiving saying, you remember my mama, sir. I believe that you do.

Oh, mercy. If she had married Roy Earl, he would still be younger than her.

Still.

Trudy cussed and lit a cigarette and went to sit on the porch, crossing her legs, bobbing her foot and slapping the flip-flop against her rough sole, rhythmic. Smoking and finally letting some tears sneak out, hot and silent and tracking down her cheeks to drip onto the weathered wood, her eyes closed, humming a Garth Brooks song in her head that had been popular back when Roy Earl was still a boy. Pretending she wasn't crying. Moths, fluttering around the yellow light covered in cobwebs and with brittle brown oak leaves trapped inside the cracked, frosted glass alongside a few flies.

Trudy.

She knew what she would do. Soon, she would go and tell Samson everything—that she wasn't happy, that she loved somebody else even if she didn't know who, and that as soon as his toe was better and his knees were right again, she would go to that person. Sounded like a plan. Enough of one for tonight.

travis latham, a general, and a vietnamese girl

An Excerpt From

At first Travis Latham thought himself in good shape in Vietnam. Better than Ronnie Ed and, far as he knew, Buddy Sykes, the other in-country boys from Edgewater County, anyway. As his tour unfolded, Travis became certain of this good fortune. Buddy, smart, a college boy, but still off in the jungle. All a big secret with Buddy. Classified.

Ronnie Ed, though? Infantry. No doubt he was in it up to his eyeballs. Travis, he felt for Ronnie Ed more than Buddy, a Lieutenant. Officers had it good, or so Travis figured.

Eventually he would understand how lucky he was being stationed at the base: He'd see grunts—muddy, filthy, haggard and stoned—stumbling out of the field and straight into the mess. Travis and his unit, who were more like medics, never looked like that—they could shower multiple times a day, if they wished. Polish their boots. It was expected of them, a discipline and order—Travis and his fellow corpsmen, well, they handled the remains.

Yeah. Hard and horrible in its own way, but not like getting shot or bombed while squatting in a mud-bog with snakes falling out of the trees on your helmet alongside the ordnance. Lots of signing off on forms, and making sure the right copy got where it need to go, and futzing around with carbon paper that leaves smudges on fingers.

Smudges. The worst of Travis's inconveniences. He made sure not to complain too loud.

Other than the details of the job, life at Da Nang Air Base, again, none too shabby: The home of MACV—Military Assistance Command Vietnam, which in its Annex of barracks Travis found himself housed—the post crawled with brass, clean-shaven and scrubbed pink, and whose pressed uniforms hung draped and spotless, with the base grounds expected to appear in similar condition at all times; the big wheels rolled through here.

A different sort of war on this base, almost a hundred miles from the DMZ. Other than handling dead bodies, Travis knew his number had come up in a manner allowing him to survive the war. It took about two weeks of handling remains before he settled down and realized it would continue to be these field soldiers, and not Travis, who would have their bodies torn apart in Vietnam. Only later would the guilt over all this luck on his part settle onto a questioning soul like bitter dew.

"You little assholes going into the infantry better stay sharp. Get your asses shot off."

Redheaded Buddy Sykes, not much older than them but already a Lieutenant, had warned Travis and Ronnie Ed one afternoon back in Tillman Falls. He'd been on leave and standing in his uniform outside The Dixiana, discoursing to the boys about the dangers of signing up for the Army as they were both intending to do, rather than waiting to be

Travis Latham, A General, and a Vietnamese Girl 221

drafted, which might not happen. "This is getting to be a hot war."

"You don't look no worse for wear." Ronnie Ed, always a smart-ass, quick with a line or a retort. "If you ask me."

"I've been to college, have an important job. I don't have to worry about the bullets and flak so much," so secret he couldn't even tell his best buddies. Buddy had studied engineering at Southeastern, so who knew what it was. Blowing up bridges. Travis had seen in movies that those guys got shot at too, so he didn't feature what Buddy Sykes meant. "And I got these bars on my shoulders. But you guys? The poets call it cannon fodder. If you ain't careful."

Neither of them had quite known what this meant. Ronnie Ed had said, if it was good enough for our Daddies, it would be fine for him, too. Buddy had shrugged and said, okay, boy. You'll find out.

Travis, as part of what became a daily ritual, peered into the latrine mirror at his face and said, "Meat. That's all," after which he bowed his head in prayer over the horrors he saw daily while assigned to the 1st Logistic Division, with an MOS designated 57-F20. Still better than getting shot. Once you saw the condition of the remains they processed, you sure as shit knew you wanted to stay far from the field:

Burnt, broken, bombed, often covered in maggots; fished out of rivers and bogs and the rich jungle, each type of remains with its own unique smell. The corpsmen all wore masks with drops of orange oil inside, but it was more Travis's ritual that made the work manageable. Taking a step back from the reality. Remains. Never 'bodies.'

Meat.

It made sense. He got assigned to Quartermaster Corps, he reckoned, because of his duties and experience back home at the IGA, to which he rose from starting as a bag boy right before he quit high school. Graves Registration—GRREG—a service with the Corps, would be his home for the duration of his tour, he said, because of internal logic:

"Typical god-damn Army—I told them I used to work in the grocery store meat department," as he explained to a group of green, glassy-eyed shavetails in the mess and fresh off the boat or plane. "Or maybe it wasn't no screw-up. You ought to see some of them grunts," which nobody wanted to hear. "They sure look like they been through a meat grinder. Better stay sharp out yonder. All I can tell y'all."

Ronnie Ed would've said that to those boys out of meanness, but Travis only wanted them to prepare themselves what they were getting into, not unlike Buddy Sykes on that day back home.

But Travis couldn't know how easy his service would be until he got there, and all during the long flights—first to California and onto a big Boeing jet that landed in Hawaii, made an unscheduled refueling stop on Wake Island, a V of coral in the middle of the vast blue Pacific, and whose runway seemed far from long enough for the big plane, both landing and takeoff an excruciating exercise in fear—he sat stove-up with tension. If he might only get on the ground and stay, Travis Latham didn't give a hoot if anybody shot at him or not.

A bumpy leg to Anderson Air Base on Guam for one last fuel top-off, and at last Cam Ranh Bay Air Base, South Vietnam, followed by several means of transport, from truck to bus to chopper, from briefings and customs and assignments and orders to land, finally, at Da Nang, wearing fresh green togs and black boots that would gain not so much as a scuff except from the rubber wheels of the gurneys Travis would later push.

On the descent to the airbase, the whole horizon to the west blazed deep, bloody red, like a magazine ad for a tropical vacation.

"That the way the sky always look over here?" Travis, pondering in his country boy drawl. "Real pretty."

A Lieutenant across the aisle snorted and said, "Private? That's the war, not a god-damn sunset."

"The war?"

"The jungle—it's burning from an airstrike. And yeah, it looks like that on a regular god-damn basis."

Travis, awed and terrified, squinted at that red band on the horizon now become a vision out of hell. Though that image remained as real as the hot part of the war would get for him, his view from on high, it would at times still land close to home.

The most vivid such instance occurred the day Travis and others watched a plane blow up while trying to land at the airfield next door. An F-4 Phantom, sputtering and wounded, its Marine pilot struggling to make it onto the ground, his engines screaming and smoking black but to no avail. They gazed, gape-mouthed and helpless, as the aircraft nosed up and exploded above the runway, raining down flaming meteors of metal. The pilot's remains, incinerated beyond recognition, had come through the morgue later that night. The dental records chumps earned their keep on that one, because everything else had been flash-fried black as char. Nasty work, gruesome and unnecessary—wasn't as though they didn't know who flew the plane. Bureaucracy. All anybody could talk about was that explosion, unlike anything most expected to see at Da Nang.

The war came home daily, however, in every black bag processed, all different, the many ways in which the deceased acquired the condition. But the remains began to run together too, once he got into the groove, noting only that groups of remains often came in with similar injuries—all with grievous mortar or gunfire wounds, else all burned, or groups missing limbs from unfortunate minefield penetrations. Ten, twelve-hour days, when it got real busy, anyway. The enormous thumping of the Chinooks, loaded down from picking up remains at the collection points. Travis would hear the racket and think, well, that's the afternoon. Word came back that we fought against some real dug-in Commie bastards back in them deep jungles. The look of the remains bore this out, but nobody said so aloud. Not around officers, anyway.

Travis got through these days by thinking of himself as a machine, mechanical arms lifting and depositing the black bags and greased, riveted claspers unzipping the remains, which were not human; he had a robot claw like on Lost in Space scratching down the information onto the smudgy carbon forms.

Travis himself was not human.

And these weren't dead American fellas like him.

Maybe when he returned home again, one day soon, all would be real and true again. For now? A stage-play of handling meat.

AFTER THE WAR heated up in '67, as Travis understood the history, the Army had set up an auxiliary processing point at

Da Nang to supplement the overwhelmed morgue in Saigon, and now two years later remains arrived mainly on the giant, thumping Chinooks, if occasionally on trucks, like today.

Tet happened over a year ago now, and while business still cooking, the flow of remains experienced interludes of quiet—long stretches, sometimes, followed by beaucoup activity. During such times of rest, corpsmen often play horseshoes along the side of the low concrete building off the airfield next to the cooler, as long as the rest of the building. At capacity it could process about a hundred-fifty sets of remains at a time, and often did.

"Latham—you hear that?"

"Damn, son." Mahoney startled Travis, queering his throw way off to the right. "Choppers?"

Blonde and skinny, Mahoney squinted into the sun. "Truck or two, sounds like."

Trucks equalled a lesser payload. Fewer remains. "Well, we got that going for us."

Travis killed time all morning tossing the horseshoes with another private, Mahoney, a kid from Boston, both smoking and shooting the shit and daydreaming about activities following the wake-up. They both sounded alien to one another, Travis reckoned. He joked with Travis about being from the south, too, which was what his neighborhood in Boston was called, Southie. A rough place, from the sound.

Travis followed Mahoney into the office and put on the smocks and got their masks and gloves ready. Corpsmen unloaded remains while Travis scratched on the clipboard and signed documents, bade the driver to countersign. The tissue-thin manifests got torn off copy by copy and further handled, hands rattling and crinkling the documents, the crucial documents, carbon paper fluttering around like the black wings of the angel of death. Drove Travis up the wall, the Army did—if you weren't processing remains, you better be stacking paperwork into unimpeachably good order.

A jeep came tearing to a stop with two officers in the back, a Major and a bird Colonel, dust and gravel in their wake back-lit by the hot Asian sun. Travis and Mahoney snapped to salute in their heavy rubber gloves they pulled on with their smocks as the brass, barely acknowledging them, bustled past them into the mortuary office.

"Some big wheels there," Travis noted to the driver as they handled the few sets of remains onto gurneys and other corpsmen bore them away. "What's the rumpus?"

"Oh, son—we brung you a General on this run," the driver said, signing the last form and pulling up the tailgate. "What you assholes think about that?"

"That don't happen every day."

Mahoney, sputtering and spooked by the news. "Shit —*them fuckers got one of our generals?*"

"Road accident. Wasn't the gooks."

"Good. There's that, at least."

"That brass, they're keeping tabs on the remains. Stay out of their way."

"Gotcha."

Accident or not, a General getting killed in the field made Travis's own blood run cold. He had gotten jumpy at what he was seeing. The frag wounds were the worst for tearing a body up, but worse still? Remains arriving after starting to putrefy in the humidity and heat of Vietnam. They had enough of those they'd adopted a protocol just for dealing with maggots. Travis decided he could get used to any part of this except for wiggle-worms. A layer of wriggling rice on a recognizable human face had the effect of making the remains seem like bodies again, a profaning, much as he would react this way back home in the meat department at the IGA. *What if the manager walked in and found vermin and insects? We be in trouble, ya'll.* A negative connotation, stomach-turning to boot.

But he didn't know what would put him over the edge, not like he had seen happen to grunts. He didn't have but a few months left by this point, though. To rotate home from this hellhole without a scratch? That was still the goal. Only outcome that mattered. Would be worth another couple of months of maggots and meat and planes exploding overhead.

Meat. This job was just handling meat. Even the General.

Travis noted a Vietnamese name coded as Civilian. "Whoa, wait—who's the dink?"

"Sweet doe-eyed little native girl." The corpsman hung out of the window of the truck. "Probably a VC kamikaze. Wouldn't surprise me."

"Why, she try to blow somebody up?"

"Not this'n. Little shits'll booby-trap you, though, if you aren't careful. Women. Little kids. Some grandmother, even. You don't ever know. She was on the main road on her scooter and ran out in front of a Gamma Goat," a six-wheeled heavy truck with a short trailer. "Ended up twisted around in the axle. Dragged her for half a click. Thought at first she was trying to bomb the convoy, but them fellas didn't find no ordnance on her. Said before it happened, she looked more scared than crazy-brave."

Travis whistled. "Guess the dental boys can skip this one."

"You axing the wrong brother." The driver, sweating running off his dark brow, cranked the truck with twin gusts of black diesel smoke. "You worry about your procedures, and I worry bout mine." They rolled up their windows and the driver ground the gears and the truck went on its way, kicking up dusty from tires covered in dried khaki-colored mud.

A FEW MONTHS EARLIER, the forensic dental identification protocol added a twist to the processing, complicated enough as it was, what with the variety of conditions: this was no normal funeral home. The areas inside the prefab, sheet-metal buildings included space for receiving, embalming, refrigeration storage, shipping, followed by the Central Identification Laboratory and the administration area, which included the Major's office. In addition, pathologists attached to the mortuary stood by to perform autopsies, and a unit tasked with conducting ballistics analysis on remains. Their data, as explained to Travis, got used to evaluate the effectiveness of enemy weapons, crucial information used in developing effective countermeasures.

Wasn't as though they couldn't manage before the new protocols, but after several mixups regarding the identity of remains at the U. S. Army Mortuary at Da Nang, a team of medical examiners had received training and assignment to document and identify every set of remains through dental records, if necessary, along with fingerprints and other available data. Another step, another set of records and documents. That's the Army for you.

You couldn't blame their unit for the screw-ups, though. Travis and the rest of the staff at the mortuary had worked with what they had, like the paperwork, and items like dog tags, all of it fallible. Unless it could talk and tell you its name and rank, dead meat often held onto its secrets.

A few weeks into the new protocols one of the dental assistants had suffered a freak-out, had gone around the bend over the condition of bodies. Mortar wounds to guts and faces had become second nature to Travis, but this poor soul had seen the first one, panicked and puked and the whole bit to the point of reassignment. Hollering about having trained to save teeth, not pry them out of corpses. A draftee, green.

Travis and Mahoney could only shrug. Besides cutting meat at the IGA, Travis worked on a farm as a boy, had gone with the farmer to a slaughterhouse and had seen blood and death before he ever got to Nam. And as Travis still said, damn, son: handling these remains still better than facing live fire in the field. They rested at night in the barracks by a damn golf course, of all places, with a foot and a half of concrete poured on one side, on the off-chance of an attack. Weren't any bullets gonna get him at Da Nang. He'd handle some meat if he had to. Suck it up, son.

The native girl on the latest run, though, her death made him feel bad. Her face, perfect and innocent and young; back of her head busted wide open, brains hanging out. So pretty that he knew someone in her village had loved and cherished her, now mourned sure as the families of the boys Travis helped send home soon would.

And indeed, the officers sniffed and poked around regarding the General which made the CO, Major Sonsini, pissed because, what? Were they saying the General's remains weren't safe here with the unit entrusted with handling remains according to the standard procedures and excelled at doing so without further supervision? Shouting and tension but it'd passed, the remains got processed, and the General returned to his place of rest in Arlington, probably. Who knew? Not Travis.

Whether native girls or generals, some days 'standard' went out the window. One time they'd had a mine-sniffing dog come in, poor critter chopped in half. His handler, crying like a baby, standing and watching them process that dog like any other soldier. Which he guessed he was. Travis grew up in the country. Respected animals, worked with them. Had had dogs. Knew what losing one felt like. None of his had got blown up, that much for sure.

The girl, though. A mangled mess, but only half of her. Her upper body, her small perfect breasts and milky skin and round face. Lips parted, eyes the same, a mask of repose that didn't match up with the pain on display in her lower extremities, her guts twisted and hanging and with road trash, straw and dust, all stuck in the viscous running fluids of her ruined body, the missing back of her skull.

"That's a pisser right there." Mahoney, hurrying Travis along. "She would've made someone a sweet little mama-san."

"Don't say that."

"Why not?"

"Because. She wasn't in no war. She made a wrong turn."

"Don't turn pussy on me now, redneck."

Travis felt pissed. This wasn't one of those typical bags of ground beef, some grunt getting his ass shot off. This, a little girl. Tried to find words, but couldn't.

Instead: "Give me that," snatching the clipboard away. With the General's processing completed and his remains removed by the other brass and their own team of corpsmen, the rest of the incoming could be processed. "We don't got all day here."

Travis scanned down the list, squinting at the row of bags, compared list to tags. At one name he froze, blinking and stupid with disbelief.

"The boys in the cooler are waiting, Latham."

Mahoney referred to the others waiting. The General's remains had thrown the schedule off, as had the dink girl. They had a whole crew working there, the corpsmen and doctors and coroners, embalmers, some of whom were civilian contractors. Big industry, the mortuary trade. The army version needed to run as efficient as a business—the processing time had been worked to a clockwork three hours, with another eight-hour period elapsing to check the embalming work. Time waited for no corpse.

"Oh, lord," Travis croaked. The clipboard, fumbled in his hands, dropped with a clatter. "Shit. Shit. Please, no."

One the notations on the manifest read:

```
PETTUS, RONALD EDWARD, Cpl.
```

Shaking, Travis went outside, Mahoney calling after him. He walked in a circle, had to remember to keep breathing.

Maybe it was another boy named that. It could be. Couldn't it? In a country big as the US? The world was full of people with the same damn names. With almost two hundred million Americans fielding a big-ass Army full of freckle-faced Ronnie Ed's, there had to be two with the same name.

But it wasn't a different Ronnie Ed, and he had had to get Mahoney to process these remains. Could not look and see for himself. Would keep on reciting it through the rest of the shift—it ain't my friend Ronnie Ed. That's how Travis got through that day and night, and yet knowing the truth.

That settled it. His ass was putting in for graveyard shift. Fewer remains came in.

"I'm sure now that ain't my boy from back home." Travis, concluding this as they went to clean and stow their heavy aprons and gloves and masks. "Some grunt with the same name. That's all."

Mahoney, lighting up a smoke and nodding. "Yeah. I'm sure that's all it is."

"Stranger shit than that's come round the bend."

"No doubt. Don't sweat it."

"I ain't. Don't you worry."

"Good on that."

And yet that night Travis drank whiskey until he puked. Got into a fight in the barracks. Slept it off without further recrimination. As he was passing out, he heard Mahoney saying, cut him a break. His buddy's remains came through today.

Drunk or not, Travis heard the remark and it brought reality home anew. He hazily recalled weeping himself into blessed unconsciousness over poor Ronnie Ed, and for his folks back home, whom he knew well from the grocery store and The Dixiana.

THE NEXT DAY and from then on, the bodies in the bags would be different. They would carry more weight. The months until he got rotated home dragged, and Travis stayed nervous like on his initial flights overseas, seeing the red sky and understanding that the stakes, the war, loomed real and dangerous. Despite handling the remains, he had let himself still believe the war wasn't all that real. When your friend comes in dead, though, no denying the reality.

How he'd face Mr. Rabbit back home, he hadn't a clue. He must never tell him. That's how. Express condolences and get on with it. Try to forget it himself.

Thinking it through every day made him sick, so much so he started spinning out the fantasy of the two Ronald Edwards, because the sickness started coming without taking another drink, and would not leave him until he got home, not until the afternoon in the bathroom of the San Francisco airport during his layover, when he took off that uniform and shoved it into the trash can. Pulled on a pair of jeans and a T-shirt he had bought, put on tennis shoes that still had Edgewater County red clay in the treads, washed his face and his body and went on like nothing had happened. No longer in that old Army anymore, but proud of his service, he reckoned, enough that nobody back home would spit on him.

Not after having to process Ronnie Ed.

Travis Latham, a mean enough redneck already, now possessed real gristle. Would whip some hippie's ass, he would. Boys were dying so them assholes could grow their hair long. Boys like Travis's best friend. Yeah. Travis peeled away the layer of that uniform and gave up pretending about Ronnie Ed. Wasn't no other way. Not once back home.

At least in Edgewater County he could ride over anytime he wished and visit the remains, interred in the Forest Knoll Garden cemetery. As the years went on, him and Buddy Sykes made a ritual out of visiting the marker. Afterwards, Travis always felt better. It was his way of making up to Ronnie Ed for pretending during the processing. For not being tough enough back at Da Nang to look his hometown boy in the eye and handle his god-durn remains the way a man—a soldier and a friend—should have done.

His brother in arms had deserved no less, and the regret would fester for life, not that Travis ever found the courage to confess to another soul, other than Buddy, or course. Having also been in war, only he could possibly understand.

acknowledgments

TRAILER TRASH — Finalist
Saturday Evening Post Short Story Award, 2013

HEROES AND VILLAINS — Winner,
South Carolina Fiction Project, 2010

EYE OF THE VANDAL — Honorary Mention,
Short Story America, 2016

about the author

Author James D. McCallister's novels, story and poetry collections contain channeled fragments from the Akashic records. A lifelong South Carolinian, he lives and loves in West Columbia alongside his wife Jenn and their beloved cats, muses all.

CONTACT THE AUTHOR AT:
www.jamesdmccallister.com

other titles from mind harvest press

FEINT
SAILING OFF THE EDGE OF THE WORLD
(Michael G. Sullivan)

DREAM WORK
(R. Bentz Kirby)

PEACE, RHODODENDRON
(Elizabeth Leverton)